SEKTION 20

Also by Paul Dowswell

Ausländer
The Cabinet of Curiosities

***

The Adventures of Sam Witchall
Powder Monkey
Prison Ship
Battle Fleet

SEKTION 20

PAUL
DOWSWELL

BLOOMSBURY

LONDON BERLIN NEW YORK SYDNEY

Bloomsbury Publishing, London, Berlin, New York and Sydney

First published in Great Britain in September 2011 by Bloomsbury Publishing Plc
49–51 Bedford Square, London, WC1B 3DP

A CIP catalogue record for this book is available from the British Library

ISBN 978 1 4088 0863 4

Typeset by Hewer Text UK Ltd, Edinburgh
Printed in Great Britain by Clays Ltd, St Ives plc, Bungay, Suffolk

1 3 5 7 9 10 8 6 4 2

www.bloomsbury.com

To
J and J
and
DLD

PROLOGUE

November 1972

Ilse Grau did not like her new job in Building Number 1 of the sprawling Normannenstrasse complex of the Stasi. She had been assured that it was a real honour to work for the boss himself – Comrade Minister Erich Mielke – but she wasn't convinced.

She didn't mind getting up early, the long trundle to work on the draughty tram, or her hot sweaty job in the kitchen, but she hated having to serve Mielke his breakfast. There was something about him that made her shiver. Maybe it was the rumour that he had been the commander of a Stalinist death squad or maybe it was the little statuette of the founder of the Soviet Secret Police he kept on his desk. Whenever she looked at Mielke's face, she felt as if she was staring into a dark, empty cellar.

She followed the instruction on preparing his breakfast, pinned to the kitchen wall.

'Two eggs, cooked for exactly four and a half minutes.'

Ilse laid out the tray precisely as the directive instructed. Serviette on the left of the egg, knife on the right. Bread, salt and pepper just so, with a smaller tray for coffee and milk.

'Get that wrong and you will be straight down to the basement, doling out slop for the cells,' her supervisor had said.

Double-checking that she had followed the instructions to the letter, she placed both trays on the only trolley in the building with wheels that went in the direction they were supposed to, and pushed it the short distance to Mielke's office.

'*Kommen Sie herein,*' he barked, and she took a deep breath and entered.

He was sitting at a plain desk with four telephones. The brown curtains behind the desk were almost identical to the ones she had in the small apartment she shared with her sister's family in Blaschkoallee. The violent red swirls of the carpet on the floor were designed more to hide the dirt than please the eye. The room smelled of furniture polish and stale sweat and tobacco. Mielke had sat at that desk since 1957 and there was now an indelible hair-oil stain on the wood panel where he sometimes leaned back to rest his head.

He smiled and held up a hand, but his eyes were devoid of sparkle. Frau Grau had never looked at his face long enough to notice but she had seen photographs. Officially approved photographs. They showed his eyes looking in two slightly different directions. It was most disconcerting.

He beckoned her to leave the tray at the side of his desk, which was already covered with the day's papers and documents. The one he held in his hand failed to interest him. Authorisation for two teenagers, recently fled to West Berlin, to be abducted and returned to East Germany where long prison sentences awaited them. They were to be eliminated if they showed the slightest resistance. Mielke approved the request in the time it took for Frau Grau to leave the room, then reached for a teaspoon to crack open an egg.

CHAPTER 1

Ten months earlier

It was Tuesday afternoon. That meant politics. It was their first lesson with Herr Würfel since the Christmas break and he was in full flow, reading a speech by General Secretary Honecker.

Alex Ostermann noticed his reflection in the classroom window next to his desk. My God, he looked bored. He tried to rearrange his features into one of earnest appreciation. He also noted, with some satisfaction, how long his hair had grown. Well over his ears and down on to his collar. He wondered how much longer he could grow it before Herr Roth, the school Principal, wrote to his parents to complain.

Beyond the window the sky was a low blanket of grey, and gusts of wind blew dead leaves to and fro in the school yard. A cold draught was seeping in through the ill-fitting window. For now, it was just enough to keep Alex from nodding off.

Herr Würfel was doing his best to keep them interested. He read Honecker's speech as though it was Goethe or Shakespeare. Words flew by: 'historical mission', 'class struggle', 'scientifically founded goals'; oft-repeated phrases that Alex barely understood.

Alex wished he was at home in his bedroom listening to music or playing his guitar, even if it was a cheap plastic one from Bulgaria. It made a loud buzz when you plugged it in and would never stay in tune. But it was a vaguely similar shape to the guitar he really wanted – a beautiful instrument of wire, wood and mother of pearl, the Gibson Les Paul. They were made in Kalamazoo, Michigan, wherever that was. Alex had learned this from a smuggled guitar catalogue which he'd pored over as keenly as other boys in the school had ogled that porn magazine Nadel's cousin had sneaked in to him from West Germany.

Alex's politics lesson had become a noise in the background, like the hum of fluorescent-tube lighting.

The noise stopped. You always noticed a noise when it stopped.

'Ostermann, what did I just say?' said Herr Würfel.

Alex hadn't got a clue.

'I'm sorry, sir,' he said. 'For a moment there I lost your thread.'

The rest of the class sniggered. Würfel turned to Nadel. 'General Secretary Honecker, sir, he said the wisdom of the working class informs the directives of the Socialist Unity Party.'

Würfel smiled proudly. Nadel was one of his star pupils. He was lined up as a possible candidate for the Stasi – the Ministry of State Security. You couldn't apply for a position there. Würfel had put Nadel's name

6

forward only last week. He hoped the recent incident with the pornographic magazine would be overlooked. After all, there were worse things than looking at naked women.

'Ostermann,' sighed Würfel, 'are we boring you? Perhaps you would like to remind us of the significance of the symbols on our national flag?'

Alex could have reeled them off in his sleep. He sat up and tried to sound enthusiastic. 'The hammer represents the workers, Herr Würfel, the wheat garland, the peasant farmers, and the compass, the intelligentsia.'

'And which are you?' smirked Würfel. 'I don't see a guitar on the flag.'

The class laughed sycophantically. Alex laughed too. He wasn't going to let Würfel make him feel small.

Würfel sighed and turned to the class. 'Now, who can tell me why the Deutsche Demokratische Republik has need for only one political party?'

A forest of hands shot up and he pointed to a girl near the front. 'Because the working class is in power there is no social or political basis for opposition,' she answered faultlessly.

As the class finished Würfel put on a record for them to listen to – a collection of marching tunes by the Band of the Ministry of State Security. Alex caught a glimpse of the record sleeve. It was the sort of sickly pastel blue you saw on most Trabant motor cars and district council railings and doors. The band stood stiff and formal on the cover photograph. *This is the music I'll have to play if I go to Hell*, he thought.

Alex had always gone to school on his bike but recently he had decided to walk. A new student in his class had caught his eye – a small, dark-haired girl called Sophie Kirsch. He knew she lived nearby and also walked to school. Alex kept hoping they would meet up.

On the way home that afternoon, he got lucky. 'Hey, Alex,' he heard a voice behind him. 'Wait for me!' They fell into step.

Sophie broke the awkward silence.

'Herr Würfel tried to make you look silly! Well, he didn't succeed.'

Alex blushed with embarrassment. 'I think I'm quite a disappointment to him,' he laughed.

'And a disappointment to us *all*,' she said with a wink. She dropped her voice to a whisper and began to mimic their teacher. 'How could you not be interested in the scientifically founded goals of the Socialist Unity Party? I think of nothing else.'

Alex laughed. He was flattered at how indiscreet she was being with him. He usually only had conversations like this with his sister or his best friends.

He searched for something to say. 'How do you like Berlin?' She had appeared in his class shortly before the Christmas break. He'd heard her family had moved from Magdeburg.

'I'm glad to be here, I suppose,' she said. 'Magdeburg was bombed to bits by the British in the war. A lot of it is still wasteland. Even more than Berlin – but there's so much more of the city here you don't notice it so much.'

Alex asked why they'd moved.

'My parents both teach at Humboldt Universität. Politics. Like Herr Würfel! I think they would get on very well. And my grandmother lives here. They wanted to be closer to her now she's getting older, to help my Auntie Rosemarie with looking after her.'

She paused and said, 'I quite like Berlin really, but it's odd being in a new town with none of your old friends around you.'

They started to talk about music. Sophie played the cello and had recently joined the school orchestra. 'Maybe I'll make some friends there,' she said. She told him she enjoyed playing the music they performed, especially the German composers – Bach, Mozart. 'It's all so elegant. It fits together so beautifully. We're good at that, aren't we,' she said. Then she lowered her voice. 'But I like rock music too.'

'Now that we're not so good at,' laughed Alex. 'But I'm trying. I play guitar a bit with my friends.'

She laughed, but neither of them felt it wise to say any more. They were discouraged from listening to Western rock music, let alone playing it. Alex was secretly thrilled that she had talked to him about it.

As they turned into Treptower Park on their journey

home, Sophie stopped to pet a pair of horses harnessed to a wooden coal wagon. On an impulse, Alex said, 'Here, come and look at this.' He took her to the vast Soviet war memorial at the heart of the park and pointed to one of the stone friezes.

A squad of Soviet soldiers, all wearing combat medals, were lined up in a ceremonial parade. One of them was kneeling before the Soviet flag, which he was holding up to kiss.

'Look,' whispered Alex, pointing for Sophie to see. 'He looks like he's blowing his nose on it.'

She burst out laughing, then Alex felt her hand on his shoulder. 'We'd better go,' she said, eyeing up the Soviet guard at the far side of the aisle, 'before Ivan there gives us a jab with his bayonet.'

As they walked home, Alex said, 'My grandma's always hated that memorial. She says the whole thing is a great big "sod off" from the Soviets to the people of Berlin. It says: "We are your conquerors. Behold our magnificence."'

Sophie gasped. 'Your granny said that?'

'In so many words,' said Alex. 'She's not very keen on the Russians.'

Sophie sensed his reluctance to say more. She respected it. You never knew, even with friends, what would get reported back. But she liked the way he had confided in her.

'I suppose someone's got to protect us from the Yanks,'

she said. 'Keep us safe from rock music and a decent pair of jeans.'

Alex felt he could trust Sophie Kirsch. He was sure she wasn't just playing along, trying to trick him into saying things that would get him into trouble with the Stasi.

The sun was going down now and a winter chill was biting through their coats. Alex said, 'We'd better get home before it rains.'

When they reached her apartment, she said, 'You know Emmy in our class?' Alex nodded. 'She's asked me to her party a week on Friday. Are you going too? It's over on Greifswalder Strasse, wherever that is.'

'Yeah, she asked me,' he said, trying to sound nonchalant. He had heard girls were put off if you seemed too keen. Alex sensed his heart beating a little faster. 'Shall I come round and collect you?' he asked.

'Yes please. It'll be nice to have someone to go with. Come at about seven? You can meet my mother and father too. That will be a treat for you both!'

Before he could answer, she'd gone.

CHAPTER 2

Alex puzzled over that remark as he walked up the six flights of stairs to his family apartment. It sounded like Sophie's mother and father were both staunch Party members. But so were his, so perhaps he shouldn't worry too much about it.

'*Guten Abend*,' he shouted, as he came into a hall cluttered with boots, coats and books. No one replied. Alex liked the old apartment where his family lived. It had three bedrooms, for a start, which meant he and his sister, Geli, had a room each. Most of his friends had to share their bedroom. And there were great high ceilings, which made the rooms seem even bigger. Alex wondered who his dad had had a quiet word with to get them in here. He wouldn't have bribed anyone. That wasn't Frank Ostermann's style. But he was always attending Party committees and conferences. He knew all the right people.

Alex helped himself to a glass of milk and some blackberry jam on rye bread, then went to his bedroom to finish his homework. His art teacher had asked them to design a house or apartment for the Deutsche Demokratische Republik of the future.

Alex spent a good hour on it before he became distracted. His room annoyed him. He was too old for his Sandman doll there on the bookshelf, but he couldn't bring himself to throw it away. He had loved the TV series when he was younger. The adventures of the red-costumed character with the white beard, usually involving a trip into space, had enthralled him. When he was ten, he was convinced he was going to be a cosmonaut. It sounded more exciting than the other career options on offer, like power station engineer or tram driver.

There were also window stickers he had only partially succeeded in scraping off: *Wattfraß*, the little devil energy-waster who reminded them to save electricity; *Rumpelmann*, the environmental campaigner who reminded them to recycle. Alex had liked these cartoon characters when he was a kid, but he'd grown cynical about them now. It was like all the stuff they told them at school about Marx and Lenin. It was just the authorities trying to control what people did.

He had started to feel like this about a lot of things he had previously accepted. It was the family car that had started it off. Everyone said how brilliant the Trabi – the Trabant – was. How it was proof that communism was best. How everyone would eventually have one and how reliable they were. But too often he had seen his father beneath the bonnet, fiddling with the engine . . .

The front door opened and broke Alex's train of

thought. He heard his sister, Geli, call hello, and went out into the hall to greet her.

She looked cross. 'How was school?' asked Alex.

She blew air through her lips. 'Not good.'

Alex didn't like to see Geli looking unhappy. He felt protective about her, even though she was two years older than him.

She had a kind face, with straight brown hair down to her shoulders and her fringe cut straight and level with her eyebrows. You might guess she was a nurse or a theology student. She wasn't as fashion conscious as some of the other girls on her photography course, and liked to wear plain black clothes and a simple black woollen coat with a silver brooch on the collar. They weren't the kind of clothes that got you noticed.

He made her a coffee as she told him what had happened.

'You know Herr Lang, my photography tutor?'

Alex had met him once and wished his own teachers were more like him.

'Well, he's gone. No explanation. But I think I know why. He'd been encouraging us to experiment with our work. "Step outside the culture of socialist realism," he said. "Not everything in art needs to glorify communism." Well, that didn't last long. They got rid of him over the holidays.'

'I'm sorry,' said Alex. 'Who's the new tutor?'

'Don't know,' said Geli. 'We find out tomorrow.'

The door opened again as their parents – Frank and Gretchen – came home together. The room filled with the aroma of alcohol and tobacco and Alex guessed they had met for a tenants' committee meeting in the local bar after work.

Gretchen had light brown hair and a rather severe demeanour. It came from years of teaching children at a polytechnic secondary school in Adlershof – one she was pleased Alex and Geli had not gone to.

Frank was a tall, handsome man with black hair and an intense, slightly forbidding air about him. He was an electrical engineer – TVs, radios, telephone exchanges . . . no one in his workplace knew more about transistors, circuits, valves and capacitors.

Drinking always made Frank a bit more cheerful. He ruffled Alex's hair. 'You need a haircut, my lad,' he said with a smile. 'Herr Roth told me at the Party committee meeting yesterday that you are starting to look like a rowdy.'

That made Alex smile. He wasn't a rowdy at all. 'Rowdy' was what people of Frank's generation called kids who vandalised bus stops and had fights in the street with rival football supporters. Kids like that would call Alex a hippy.

'We need to tidy up a little,' said Gretchen decisively. 'Grandma is coming to tea.'

Grandma Ostermann was a stout and rather formidable-looking woman. Everything about her was curves – even the round felt hat that fitted snugly on her head over her round wrinkled face.

Alex and Geli had a soft spot for their grandma. She complained about how scruffy they were, but she always brought lovely chocolates back from her trips to West Berlin. Much better than the stodgy chocolates they could get, which tasted like they were made from lard.

The authorities didn't mind old people going across the Wall to the other side. They didn't even care if they stayed. It was the young and the workforce who were forbidden to travel to the West.

A loud knocking at the door heralded Grandma's arrival. She stood huffing and puffing from her climb up the stairs. '*Um Gottes Willen!*' she said. 'Why can't you live in a bungalow?'

She came into the living room, banged down a bag of West German coffee on the dining table, then immediately demanded that they close the curtains so that she didn't have to look at the Soviet war memorial, which they could see through the window.

She turned to Alex and did what she always did when she came to the apartment: tugged on his hair. 'You still have your girly locks! No girlfriends yet, I imagine. Especially looking like that!'

Alex laughed. He wasn't going to take the bait.

Then she asked Geli, 'And how is Jan-Carl?'

Jan-Carl was Geli's boyfriend. Frank and Gretchen liked him. He was a project supervisor in the East Berlin machine tool industry. Geli had been more reckless in her choice with previous boyfriends, especially the one a couple of years ago who had distributed anti-Stasi leaflets he'd made on a child's toy printer, but fortunately the authorities had taken no action against Geli on that occasion. She'd even managed to get into the local *Oberschule* to study for a place at technical college.

Geli smiled and told her grandma Jan-Carl was fine. Recently though, she'd been having her doubts about him. Especially as he made a habit of referring to her photography as her 'little hobby'.

After they'd eaten, Frank and Gretchen insisted they miss their usual Tuesday night *Star Trek* on the Western TV. They would watch the East German channel instead. The family had missed the New Year TV spectacular earlier in the week and it was being repeated that evening. *Ein Kessel Buntes* – a Kettle of Colour – it was called.

'More like a kettle full of crap,' muttered their grandma under her breath. She detested that sort of thing. Alex and Geli exchanged a knowing look. It was their parents' ploy to get her to go home early.

Before the programme started there was an advert for the Wartburg – the larger and more desirable East German alternative to the Trabi.

'Can we get one of those, Vati?' teased Alex. 'Perhaps it'll break down less!'

Frank laughed. 'You have to wait ten, fifteen years for a Wartburg.'

The advert continued to extol its virtues '. . . and enough space in the boot for fifty-seven footballs.'

Alex said, 'Why would anyone want fifty-seven footballs?' and Grandma chuckled and dug him in the ribs with her elbow.

Ein Kessel Buntes began with the sort of music that had been popular in the mid-sixties – a big brass arrangement with a rock and roll backbeat. Then there were dancers in top hats and sparkly jackets and stockings and high lace-up boots that were supposed to look sexy. They started to prance around in formation, singing about 'starting something'. It could have been a romance by the way they were making eyes at the camera. But if you listened closely they were talking about starting a better life in the DDR. Then the camera cut from the studio to the same dance company in the great concrete shopping centre of Alexanderplatz, with the TV Tower in the background.

'Proud of it, aren't they,' said Alex sarcastically. His parents ignored him.

Alex hated that tower. A great silver sphere perched on a slender stem, it had been opened last year and hailed as living proof that the DDR was the technological equal to any of the capitalist nations. You couldn't get away from it. It was visible from every part of the city, east or west. Alex thought it looked like an enormous malevolent eyeball.

Grandma Ostermann understood. She cackled. 'They couldn't even get that right. The bottom half looks like a

18

chemical works chimney and the top half looks like it's been stolen from a power station.'

Frank and Gretchen shifted uncomfortably on their sofa. Grandma continued to needle them.

'And that cross you can see at sunset. Oh dear . . .'

The tower had a design flaw that caused the sign of a cross to be reflected on the sphere high above the city whenever the evening sun caught it. They had heard the architect had been sent to prison for that. Alex wondered if he'd done it deliberately or if it was just an unlucky accident.

'Do you want Alex to walk you home, Mutter?' said Frank.

'*Nein, danke,*' she said with a smile. 'Alex is a skinny thing. I would have to protect him if we ran into trouble.' She got up to leave.

'I'll come anyway,' said Alex. He'd had enough of *Ein Kessel Buntes* too and he wanted to stretch his legs.

'The Russians aren't that bad, are they?' he asked as they walked along the edge of the park. They could see the brightly lit war memorial through the bare trees. 'They got rid of the Nazis, didn't they?'

'They stripped our country bare,' she said. 'Whole factories. The rails and sleepers from the train lines. Our best scientists . . . and our soldiers. When your grandfather came back from his Russian prison camp after the war, he was skin and bone. You could hardly recognise him. No wonder he died young.'

19

Alex liked the way his grandma said what she thought. When they were alone, she would remark scornfully how much the DDR was like the Third Reich. 'They think they're 180 degrees apart,' she snorted. 'But just look at them. Free German Youth, just like Hitler Youth; the Stasi, just like the Gestapo; Bautzen, just like Dachau. If they hadn't built the Wall to keep everyone from escaping, there'd just be the Stasi and a handful of Socialist Unity Party *Dummköpfs* left in the country. You watch how you go, young Alex. You don't want them to take an interest in you.'

Alex noticed that his grandma was being more serious than usual. You weren't forced to do things as people had been under the Nazis. Like you didn't *have* to join the youth groups, but everyone knew you ought to be in them if you wanted to get on. You'd still have a job, of course, after you left school if you didn't – everyone in the DDR had a job – but maybe you could look forward to being a shovel store assistant or a broom cupboard monitor rather than head of building projects for the Leipzig urban district.

Alex returned home, hoping to catch the last of *Star Trek* with Geli. He was disappointed. Their parents were listening to General Secretary Honecker giving a speech about how the DDR was building four-hundred thousand homes a year and that by 1990 every family in the country would have their own home.

Alex didn't like Comrade Honecker at all. He was like

some unpleasant, pompous uncle. The sort who patted you on the head, spoke too loudly and never listened to what you actually said. Just looking at him, Alex could tell he smelled of mothballs and those cough tablets that tasted like they were made out of tar.

CHAPTER 3

Alex liked Thursdays – that was the evening his band got together to play after school. His parents allowed his friends to practise in their apartment. The Ostermanns lived on the top floor and the neighbours downstairs didn't get home until after six.

They sat around in the living room. Alex played his Bulgarian electric guitar through an old gramophone. Frank had taken some wires from inside and connected them to a socket for Alex to plug into.

There were a couple of other lads from his year at school – Anton and Holger. Both had cheap acoustic guitars, although they claimed to be saving up for electric ones. Anton was blonde and stocky. Holger was dark and skinny, and his girlfriend, Effi, said he looked like Keith Richards.

Anton played the bass parts on his guitar. Alex suspected he might be tone deaf – so he was happy to just play the single notes his role required. Holger was as good as Alex, and was always asking to borrow his electric guitar. Although Holger was a good friend, Alex sometimes wished he hadn't asked him to join. He took too much attention from him.

The drummer, Heinz, was a couple of years younger. Unlike the rest of them, who had the shaggiest mops of hair their school and parents would allow, Heinz had the sort of short back and sides the army would approve of. He played in the trumpet and drums brigade of the local Free German Youth and he was always pestering the youth leader to let him borrow the snare drum he used in parades. But Heinz had been told he was not to use their equipment to play any rock music nonsense, especially with a bunch of rowdies like Alex, Holger and Anton. So for now, Heinz had his own drumsticks and a set of tins and boxes.

'We need a name,' said Holger, before they had played a note.

'I've got a couple,' said Anton. They all looked at him warily.

'Purple Fog,' he said, eyes wide with expectation.

The others said nothing.

'All right then. Troll Matrix.'

'They're both crap,' said Alex.

Anton pretended to look hurt. 'I suppose you want to call us the Alex Ostermann Experience,' he teased.

Alex laughed. 'Well, it does have a certain ring to it!' Actually, he thought that was pretty cool. It was his group after all. He had got the thing off the ground and he was the one with an electric guitar.

'How about Freak Power?' said Holger. It was a phrase he had come across watching West German television

– on a placard carried by some hippies at a Vietnam War demonstration.

'Cool,' said Alex. 'I can live with that.'

Heinz snorted with impatience. He wondered why he was so much smarter than these *Dummköpfs* when he was two years below them at school. 'I'll never get to borrow a snare drum for a group called Freak Power. We'll have the Stasi banging down the door before we get to the first chorus.'

They only needed a name if they did any gigs and they were a long way off that. 'I've got a new song,' said Alex, changing the subject. 'Want to hear it?' They all nodded. 'No words yet, but I've got the tune.'

The rehearsal went OK. They played Alex's new song until they got bored with it. When they stopped for a break, Anton pulled out a leaflet for a school talk. 'Here, look at this,' he scoffed. The talk was called '*Zuverlässiger Schutz des Sozialismus*' – the Reliable Protection of Socialism – and had a photograph of Honecker to illustrate it. It was an official portrait they all recognised. He had a smug smile on his face, which didn't quite go with his blank, dead eyes.

'He looks like he's just farted in a crowded room and he's trying to keep a straight face about it,' snickered Anton. They all laughed and Alex thought he was lucky to be in the company of friends who all trusted each other.

They managed to get through 'Back in the USSR' without Anton forgetting his bass line. They even sounded pretty good doing the harmonies. They thought that would be a fine one to do if the Stasi ever came to listen. Then they played 'Jumpin' Jack Flash' – the Rolling Stones song. There was something about this music that gave Alex a visceral thrill. Singing these songs made his heart beat faster in a way the school choir could never do.

The downstairs neighbours came home early and the boys soon started to hear banging coming up through the floorboards. 'I'd hate to see the dents in that ceiling,' said Alex.

'Next week we shall have a name,' announced Holger portentously. 'Otherwise we *will* be called Freak Power.'

The rest of them laughed that off and all agreed to meet again the following Thursday.

CHAPTER 4

Herr Würfel poured another cup of strong black coffee in a bid to liven himself up. He was using the final ten minutes of the morning break to work on assessments for his year group. The one for Alex Ostermann was taking some effort.

```
Treptow Polytechnic School

Year 10 Group Assessment

From: Year Group Leader

To: Principal

Ostermann is a dangerously overconfident
youth with an inflated idea of his own
importance and amusement value. He
disrupts the harmony of the group and his
behaviour is a direct challenge to the
ideal of the new socialist personality.

He refuses to take his political
responsibilities seriously and his slyly
```

```
mocking attitude towards the SED is a
cause for serious concern.
```

Würfel was always looking for an excuse to discipline
Alex. But he could never pin anything on him. He always
received a polite response but there was a twinkle in the
boy's eyes that made Würfel feel he was being mocked.
This anger rose to the surface as he typed.

```
He has a questioning intelligence and is
popular with his peers — but this makes
him an even more insidious influence.
```

Outside in the yard, where the pupils were waiting in the
cold for the break to end, he could hear a group of them
roaring with laughter. He looked out of the window to see
Alex Ostermann surrounded by admirers. Through the
open window he could hear Alex singing a song. It was
obviously one he had made up – a parody of a drinking
song, the sort the older generation would sing when
they'd sunk a few beers.

Alex's mates roared with laughter. Herr Gersten, the
elderly school caretaker, had already complained about
him that morning. Perhaps Alex was mocking the old
man now? He carried on writing.

```
Despite his 'gang leader' personality there
are no recorded incidents of his using his
```

```
position to bully or humiliate the less
popular children. He does, however, make a
habit of mocking the school authorities,
from teachers to caretaker.
```

Würfel asked himself if he was being unfair. Did he dislike Alex because he seemed to be having the happy school days Würfel had never had? Most people liked Alex. He didn't want Herr Roth, the Principal, to start to question his judgement. He knew Roth was a close friend of Alex's father, Frank. And at least Alex hadn't been burping the National Anthem, like that wretched boy Anton Brauer. That had earned him a well-deserved visit from the Stasi. Würfel began to feel magnanimous and rewrote his third paragraph.

```
In mitigation, he has a questioning
intelligence and is popular with his
peers . . .
```

He finished with a flourish.

```
. . . and with the correct application of
remedial persuasion and guidance I
believe we can still hope he will mature
to become a useful and productive member
of the DDR.
```

That would do. There was no sense in ruining someone's life quite this early in the day.

Alex was really pleased with his design for future housing in East Germany. It had been a while since he'd actually enjoyed a school project. Sitting in the art room before the teacher arrived, he listened to the class discussing their work. Most of them, it seemed, had designed apartments exactly like the ones that were going up on building sites all over East Berlin. Alex's, though, was a bulbous structure on the end of a great curved staircase. It had an organic feel about it, like a tulip on a stalk. Everyone would have their own space and no neighbours to annoy them.

Fräulein Bachmeier, the art teacher, arrived in her usual brown nylon dress. Although she was quiet and a bit severe, Alex thought she was quite pretty, even in her black-rimmed spectacles, and he wanted to impress her.

Fräulein Bachmeier went through all their work in turn, showing it to the class and passing swift and blunt judgement. Alex's illustration did not please her. It expressed bourgeois individualist tendencies, she declared. Further work like this, she warned him in front of the entire class, would see him marked down in his exams.

'How are we going to win our housing battle by 1990 with ideas like that?' she said.

Alex tried to hide his humiliation with an unconvincing smile.

She turned to Stefan and held up his project with a look

of warm approval. Alex always thought Stefan was prime Party material and was careful what he said to him.

'All the components are the same, so the production will be cheap and easy,' she told the class. 'And they are duplicated over ten floors so the minimum space can be used for the maximum number of dwellings. And look how Stefan has created a three-quarter square with all dwellings overlooking a common play area. Here all the mothers can look out of their windows and see if their children are playing safely in the designated area.'

Stefan lit up with pride.

'Alex, you must think in a more socialist direction,' she added sternly. 'After all, when all your needs are met – that's socialism. And "all your needs" means a proper apartment for all, with hot and cold water and its own bathroom and lavatory.'

Alex could see her point, but that just made him feel even more despondent.

'When all your needs are met . . .' Fräulein Bachmeier was relieved to have got that little phrase in. The Principal had told them in the staffroom on Monday morning that this was to be the political slogan of the week. They should try to include it in as many lessons as possible.

Alex's morning did not improve. Next was a careers guidance tutorial with Herr Walter. Alex had said several times he intended to teach, but recently Herr Walter had been steering him away from that idea. So now Alex said he wanted to be a musician.

His tutor scoffed. 'Alex, you are a guitar player. There are no guitars in the state orchestra.'

Alex protested. 'Everyone likes what I play in the school concerts and in the yard at break.'

Herr Walter shook his head. 'If you could play Bach's preludes and sonatas, that would be something. But you can only play pop music. That is not a skill that will further the future of socialism.'

Alex tried to look as clueless as he could. That always annoyed his careers tutor.

Herr Walter grew exasperated. 'Just look at all these leaflets.' He gestured at the wall.

'Look! Bricklaying, mining, construction, working with economically useful animals . . . you have such a wide choice. And if you apply yourself, you could even become an architect or a chemist. There'll always be work for chemists. Our chemical industry is one of the best in the world. I know you're clever, Alex, so stop pretending to be stupid.

'I had a boy like you five years ago. In the end he joined a brigade of builders, and we're now in the midst of the greatest building campaign in our nation's history. You should see the medals he's won for his brigade . . .'

Alex was no longer listening. In his head, he was trying to work out the fingering on 'Honky Tonk Women' by the Rolling Stones, and wondering why he could never get it to sound like them. One of his mates had told him you had to tune the guitar differently. Alex had never thought of that.

Seeing Alex's gaze had settled somewhere between the window and infinity, Herr Walter sighed. 'Alex, you are trying my patience. Please go. And when I see you again, I expect you to have read at least four of these leaflets and arrived at a sensible decision about the area in which you would like to pursue your career.'

He watched Alex leave with a mounting sense of impatience, then reached for a progress form and began to scribble rapidly.

Alex walked back to the school canteen hoping to catch up with Anton and Holger. He was not worried about his future. He might not be in his local Free German Youth group any more, but he was always doing the things they were supposed to do – taking newspapers for recycling, going to the local nursing home to sing with his guitar. When the time came to find a job, his father knew all the right people. And how could he really know what he wanted to do for the rest of his life at his age?

Anton gave him a cheery wave. 'Holger's not in today,' he said. 'Probably decided to stay in bed and dream up more names for the group.'

Geli had not had a good morning either. The new photography tutor, Herr Fuhrmann, kept telling them their art was a tool to perfect the socialist state. 'After all, when all your needs are met – that's socialism,' he told them.

What had that got to do with photography? thought Geli.

At breaktime she got out a copy of the fashion magazine *Sybille* and sat on her own with a coffee. They never published enough of them and Geli had been waiting for weeks to borrow it. She turned to a series of shots by Ute Mahler, which had a powerful, melancholy feel. A beautiful model was standing thigh deep in a lake at dawn, her hair and clothes drenched with chilly water. Nothing in this photograph said anything great and glorious about the DDR.

Geli's class project was also subversive, in its own quiet way. She was fascinated by the ruins of old buildings – the ones that had survived the Industrial Revolution, the First World War and then the rise of Hitler. She wondered what these buildings had seen. Who had lived in them? *'Na und?'* – Who cares? – said Jan-Carl. But Geli did.

One she photographed recently had caught the eye of Herr Lang, her old tutor. She had shot this grand wreckage of the past at first light one frosty December morning. Snow had fallen in the night and a mist hung in the air. The snow settled on the bare struts of the ruined roof and the entire building looked damp and decayed.

That house held so many stories – which was why it made such an evocative picture. Herr Lang told her it was the best photograph she had ever taken.

She suspected Herr Fuhrmann would not like it very much but she had an explanation lined up for him.

'It portrays the decay of the old system,' she told him.

'Ach, Ostermann,' he chided. 'You need to do something that lifts the spirits, not wallow in the past.'

He lowered his voice and tried to sound avuncular, although his advice was too bald to be anything other than a warning. 'I detect harmful tendencies in your work, Fräulein Ostermann. You must think more carefully about the subjects of your photographs. Your work should celebrate the socialist spirit.'

She tried to hide her disappointment and wondered what else she could get away with doing. Perhaps she could photograph the triumphs of the socialist paradise. The Trabis, the concrete wastelands of the new estates, the windswept shopping centre at Alexanderplatz. She would need an especially overcast day for that.

Alex asked Geli to drop by his school at the end of the day and meet him in the canteen. He had told her about Sophie and wanted to introduce her. As the three of them wandered out of the entrance hall, they passed a table covered with leaflets. Nadel and some other eager students were handing them out. This was how you got to be one of the leaders of the future, thought Alex. He wondered how he'd feel about having someone like Nadel or Stefan lecture him about the need for greater asphalt production one day.

Alex read out the title of the nearest leaflet: *The Marxist-Leninist Blueprint for a New World*. 'Thanks,' he said, taking one from Nadel with a cheery smile. 'I'll read it if I get insomnia!'

As they walked home, Alex was pleased that Sophie and Geli seemed to be comfortable with each other. As they passed by Treptower Park, Geli saw a familiar face among a group of kids in tracksuits. She called out. 'Hey, Lili!'

'Who's that?' said Sophie. 'I think I recognise her.'

'This is the famous Lili Weber,' said Alex, as Lili came over to greet them. 'Lili – star of stage, screen and swimming pool!'

Lili blushed. 'Hi, Alex.'

'You're the swimmer, aren't you?' said Sophie. 'I've seen you on the television. So how do you know a rowdy like Alex?'

Lili looked a little affronted and Sophie realised she had said the wrong thing.

'Geli and I were at school together,' Lili said. Her voice was unusually gruff and Alex wondered if she had a cold. 'They are my friends.' Then she smiled. 'It's been ages since we met.'

They talked about her training and the sports academy she had been going to for the last couple of years. 'Swimming, swimming, swimming,' said Lili, 'politics, and then more swimming. I feel like I'm turning into a fish.'

Her voice had a touch of anger although she tried to pass it off as a joke. 'But it's the Olympics this year. All very exciting!'

The others were waving at her and calling her back. 'All right,' she called out. 'I'm coming.' Then she turned to her friends and smiled apologetically. 'I'd better go or I'll miss the coach back. Let's meet up soon!'

They carried on walking home. 'We've known Lily since we were tiny,' said Geli. 'She's always been a brilliant swimmer.'

Meeting a sports star had made Sophie feel quite excited, even if Lili had been a little brusque with her. She enjoyed being with Alex and Geli. She felt like she could say what she wanted to them. 'Look at this,' she sniggered, as they passed an ill-lit clothes shop window. 'East Berlin, fashion capital of the world!'

The shop had done its best to make the most of their display, but the window was far too big for the goods they had on offer. Three flimsy nighties made from some scratchy man-made fabric in a dull pastel blue sat on spindly, headless mannequin torsos. A pale pink corset with conical protuberances at the bust made up the tableau.

Further along the street there were a few parked cars but as the winter evening drew in everything was empty and still. There was nothing going on, thought Alex. Nothing at all.

CHAPTER 5

Alex trudged carefully through a light snowfall to drop by Holger's apartment on the way to school. Alex hadn't seen him since the band had last played together and he wanted to know if he was coming to the next rehearsal. Holger's mother answered the door and Alex could tell at once something bad had happened.

'*Guten Tag, Frau Vogel*,' said Alex. 'What's happened? Is Holger ill? I've brought him a bar of chocolate.'

'We thought you were the Stasi,' she said. 'Come to tell us the worst. We haven't seen him since Saturday afternoon. Nor Effi.'

Alex liked Holger's girlfriend, but Effi was so outspoken in her dislike of the DDR he didn't like being seen with her in public. Even Holger would shush her when they were in cafés or the sort of bars that served teenagers. Alex was glad she didn't go to his school.

'Have they escaped?' whispered Alex. 'Gone over the Wall?'

She stared, unblinking. 'That would seem the most likely explanation.'

Alex felt hurt. Holger was his friend. He thought he

might have told him, even if it was just to say goodbye. He bit his tongue. Holger's mother had gnawed her nails to the quick and had the ghostly pallor of someone who had not slept properly for several days.

'I'm so sorry,' said Alex. 'Can you let me know if you hear anything?'

Alex walked away with a heavy heart. The Wall was close enough to Treptower to hear the guards dogs there howling in the night. They said they kept them hungry to make them vicious. Along with the dogs, he'd heard, there were mines, machine guns, mantraps, and guards who would shoot to kill. The mere thought of the Wall filled him with dread. At school the teachers called it the Anti-Fascist Protective Barrier and told them it had been constructed to prevent an attack from West Germany and to hinder the activities of West German provocateurs. Alex didn't think many people really believed that.

He had only glimpsed the Wall from a distance. All areas adjoining it were designated *Verboten* – Forbidden. You had to have a good excuse – work or residence – to be anywhere near it. There were always plenty of patrols to stop you and ask questions. If you had no good reason to be there, you were an immediate suspect.

On the other side of the street two men in heavy overcoats were sitting in a beige Wartburg, watching the comings and goings at Holger's apartment. This was their first bit of action since midnight. One of them wiped the condensation from the passenger window, removed his thick gloves, and pointed a camera at Alex Ostermann as he emerged from the apartment block stairwell. 'That's something to show for seven hours of freezing our arses off,' he muttered.

Across the city Unterleutnant Erich Kohl's working day was just beginning. Like his freezing colleagues in Treptower, Kohl worked for the Stasi. Unlike his colleagues, he was comfortably warm. As he drove his Mercedes saloon up to the Invalidenstrasse border crossing into West Berlin, the snow was turning to sleet and he was grateful for the efficient heating system the car provided.

He was so used to his excursions into the West he rarely felt nervous about going through a checkpoint. All he had to do was drive over on a fake pass. The West German border guards rarely took much interest in anyone coming over from the East, especially if it looked like they were returning to the West.

Getting back to East Berlin would be no trouble at all. The guards would be alerted. No questions would be asked. There would be no delays and the car would most definitely not be stripped down for a thorough search. This frequently happened to Westerners, to deter them from visiting, and it had happened to Kohl once as he returned from an assignment. The guards got the scolding of their life and their commanding officer was transferred to a catering depot close to the Polish border.

Kohl's aliases were always well prepared, and he picked a

different crossing point every time, so the West German guards would be less likely to get to know his face. Today he was Reinhardt Schoenberg, resident of Charlottenburg, insurance salesman, on his way back from a visit to relatives in the East. They waved him through without a second glance. Kohl was good at aliases. He'd had a lot of practice.

He'd been handsome once – the classic tall dark stranger – but nowadays, whenever he caught his reflection in the window of a night tram, the puffy, double-chinned face that stared back filled him with gloom. He sometimes bought shampoo on his trips to the West that promised to make his lank greasy hair look shiny and full-bodied, but that was beyond even the magic of Nivea.

Today he had a meeting set up in Hannover, in West Germany. It was a long drive but he didn't mind. He liked the Mercedes they had given him. It was a hell of a lot more comfortable than his Trabi, which pootled along like a lawnmower. When you put your foot down on the *Autobahn*, it really took off. Everything about it was better. It even had an eight-track music centre in the dashboard so you could listen to your own music if you got bored with the radio. That was fantastic. Like having your own radio station where you told the DJ what to play. The Mercedes had the sort of comfort that only top Party officials could expect in the East. In the West it was perfect for his anonymous middle-class-professional persona.

His job was a great game and he was good at it. And the West had all those shops bursting with everything you could ever want, and more of anything than you would ever actually need. But the people he had to deal with filled him with disgust. His current assignment was especially trying – making contact with a group of supposed revolutionaries who called themselves the Red Army Faction. They had started to make the news with some regularity now, although the Western media usually referred to them as the Baader-Meinhof Gang, after two of their leading lights.

So far the Red Army Faction had burned down a couple of department stores, carried out a few bank robberies and killed a couple of cops. The Stasi had funded a visit to Palestinian training camps in the Middle East for them and now the Faction wanted to know if they would provide arms, grenades and explosives so they could take their fight to the streets.

Kohl had already met two of them in Munich – a man and a woman – and had gone back to his commander and recommended extreme caution. They were spoiled rich kids, playing with guns and political attitudes to shock their parents, he reported. He felt vindicated when a contact in the West German secret service informed them that the couple had been arrested a week after the meeting. They had been speeding in a stolen car and were stopped by the police. Their aliases didn't stand up. Amateurs.

But word came down to Kohl from the boss to forge strong links with the Red Army Faction. Anything that discredited or destabilised the West German state was to be encouraged. So here he was now, ready to meet another bunch and wondering what he was letting himself in for.

He reached his destination in the early afternoon – a residential apartment block in one of Hannover's smarter suburbs. A young man with a ponytail and a tie-dye T-shirt answered the door. Kohl took an instant dislike to him.

The antipathy was mutual. 'Herr Schoenberg, I have to tell you we are disappointed to see you. We let it be known that we would have preferred to deal with another operative. There are several people in our organisation who hold you responsible for the arrest of our two comrades in Munich.'

Kohl tried to control his anger. 'There are no grounds at all for that fanciful conclusion,' he snapped.

He tried to be more placatory. 'Rest assured their detention was nothing to do with the Ministry of State Security. We are not amateurs, Herr . . . ?' Kohl raised an inquisitive eyebrow to ascertain his contact's surname.

'You may call me Klaus,' said the man brusquely. 'You must know our procedures. My comrades will be arriving shortly.'

But they didn't. Kohl and his contact spent a sullen couple of hours in virtual silence, staring out at the occasional flurries of snow that danced outside the window. Kohl maintained an icy calm. He was beginning to think his journey had been futile.

The phone rang. Klaus nearly leaped out of his skin.

He snatched it up and Kohl heard an angry voice in the earpiece. Klaus turned to glare at Kohl.

'There are several suspicious people in the streets around the apartment block,' he said. 'My comrade is convinced they are plain-clothes police. Are you sure you weren't followed into the building?'

Kohl stared at the man without replying.

'I told them we should never have trusted you,' said Klaus. 'How do we know you won't betray us? Maybe the secret service know your face?'

Kohl could feel the weight of his pistol in his jacket pocket and had to restrain himself.

They were interrupted by the sound of a key in the door. A young woman wearing sunglasses, a large hat and a mini skirt, burst through the door.

She started when she saw Kohl. 'Who is he?' she demanded.

'They sent him over from the East. He's supposed to be helping us,' said Klaus. 'So where the hell have you been?'

'I was supposed to meet Ralf and Brigitte but they didn't show up.'

'They rang just now,' snapped Klaus. 'Did you notice anything odd out there? Were you being followed?'

'Of course not,' she snapped back at him. 'What did Ralf say?'

'They thought we were being watched. There are suspicious people hanging around outside.'

She shook her head and shrugged.

'You shouldn't have come here,' Klaus said to her. 'You're putting the operation in danger. If Ralf and Brigitte were being trailed, then so are you . . .' Klaus was almost hysterical in his exasperation.

The woman seemed indifferent to his concern. Instead, she turned on Kohl. 'And what the hell are we doing collaborating with jumped up neo-Nazis like the Stasi?'

Kohl was shocked that a woman – a girl – felt she could be so opinionated.

'And how do we know *he* won't betray us?' the girl added. 'How do we know he hasn't tipped off the cops?'

Kohl had had enough. These people were inept. It was time to go. He got out his gun and swiftly screwed his silencer to the barrel. The two of them stopped arguing only when he was pointing his weapon directly at them.

'Shut up,' he said brusquely. 'I'm sure your neighbours are finding your conversation of great interest.'

Klaus went white. 'They are out during the day,' he managed to stammer. Kohl noticed with some distaste that he had wet himself. He clearly thought he was going to kill him. The girl was made of sterner stuff but she was still doing her best to stop her hands from shaking.

Kohl moved the barrel of his gun from one to the other, relishing his power. 'Take off your clothes,' he said. They both looked aghast. 'Quickly,' he ordered.

They hurriedly stripped, the girl bravely muttering that he was a pervert. That made Kohl smile. He had completely lost his trust in these people. He wanted to leave the apartment quickly, anonymously and alive and he did not want them following him.

'You.' He turned to Klaus. 'Give me your keys and put all of your clothes in that.' He pointed to a plastic bag on the coffee table.

'What, all of them?' said Klaus, with a look of terrified disbelief on his face.

'Just the ones you've been wearing, you *Arschloch*,' said Kohl.

While they gathered their clothes, Kohl knocked the phone off the table and crushed it into several pieces with his boot.

He stepped towards the door with the bag. 'You may tell your organisation I had nothing to do with the arrests of your comrades. And whatever has happened today is, likewise, entirely down to your own stupid bungling.'

He left, swiftly double-locking the door behind him, then despatched the bag of clothes, the keys, and his gun, down the apartment rubbish chute. He did not want to be carrying a gun if he was stopped by the police. By the time his captives had pulled on a fresh set of clothes and found a spare set of keys, Kohl was halfway down the adjacent street and taking the keys for his Mercedes from his pocket. As he drove off, a man in a plain grey coat and a black patch over his right eye watched the car turn towards the city's ring road. When the Mercedes moved out of view, he spoke into a small two-way radio transmitter.

* * *

It was dark now and the headlights of Kohl's Mercedes were picking out flecks of sleet amidst the persistent rain. He rubbed his tired eyes and squinted at the road ahead. If he kept going, and the snow held off, he should be home by midnight.

Kohl pulled deep on a Marlboro. He liked these American cigarettes, although he would never dream of smoking them in front of his colleagues. He had promised himself a coffee before he crossed over but he couldn't shake off the feeling that he was being followed.

Had he had a lucky escape? Had there really been plain-clothes police around the building? Or had his contacts just been smoking too much cannabis and were overcome with paranoia?

Maybe it was because he was tired, but Kohl could feel himself getting increasingly angry. He felt a real, deep hatred for these young people – hippies all of them – and the ones in East Germany who wanted to be like them. In his day you joined the *Hitler-Jugend* or the *Bund Deutscher Mädel* and you did what you were told.

The young were meant to be the fighting reserve of the Party. If that was the case, then God help them. Even the kids who were in the Free German Youth seemed to want to grow their hair and listen to pop music. That was OK these days, he had been told, although there were limits on what was permissible. They had been infected, all of them. But it was the ones who really let their hair grow and listened to the banned music and never attended youth meetings, they were the ones who were a real cancer in the Republik.

CHAPTER 6

Anton came running up to Alex in the lunch break. 'Effi's been arrested. Her parents told me they'd had the Stasi round. She's in Hohenschönhausen.'

They'd all heard of that. It was a detention centre in the east of the city.

'And there's been a shooting at the Wall,' said Anton. 'Heard it on the Western news the other day. Didn't think much about it until I heard Holger had gone missing.'

Alex went cold. Anton's excitement was unsettling. And he was being very indiscreet. 'It's got to be them,' Alex whispered. 'Did you know they were going?'

Anton shook his head. He held up his fingers to count the options. 'He's either dead, injured, in custody, or got away. What do you think?'

Alex walked away without replying.

He went to Holger's apartment as soon as school was over. His mother answered the door again, but only opened it a few centimetres. 'Don't come here again, Alex,' she whispered through the crack in the door. 'We've had the Stasi here. I don't know what's happening.' Then she broke down, and her words came out in breathless sobs. 'They won't tell us anything . . .'

The door shut and Alex walked home, trying to fight back his own tears. It was not surprising he failed to notice the beige Wartburg and the man inside who pointed a camera at him.

The next morning the school secretary summoned Alex from a maths lesson and ordered him to report to the Principal's office. He was sure this was about Holger, and as he walked the short distance down the corridor he felt grateful to his friend for not telling him about his plans to escape. Now he could go in and claim with transparent honesty that he knew nothing.

Two middle-aged men, in nondescript suits and severe haircuts, were sitting at the Principal's desk. They motioned for him to sit and fixed him with piercing stares.

Alex gave a cautious smile and asked them how he could help. They continued to stare and Alex began to feel the sweat run down his back.

'You are a known accomplice of the border violator, Holger Vogel,' said one of them.

So, it was definitely true. Holger had tried to escape.

'Holger is my friend,' said Alex. 'I know he has disappeared because his mother told me. But I know nothing about border violations.'

The questions came rapidly and alternately from the two men.

'You are aware that border violation is one of the most serious crimes?'

'Yes, sir.'

'And do you swear that the border violator never mentioned his intentions before he committed this crime?'

'No, sir.'

'You were aware? Do you mean he did mention this?'

'No, sir, he never spoke to me about it.'

'And are you aware that assisting a border violator is a crime almost as serious as border violation itself?'

'Yes, sir.'

'Did you suspect at any time that Vogel harboured any negative delusions about the DDR?'

'Did he ever voice such delusions to you?'

Alex was getting confused.

'I am happy to swear to you both that I never heard Holger say anything about his escape plans . . .'

'Escape?' said one of the men angrily. 'This is not an *escape*.' He spat out the word. 'It is a betrayal by a traitor to his country. Your usage indicates a harbouring of false opinions. Have *you* ever considered "an escape", as you put it?'

Alex did his best to keep the fear from his voice.

'No, sir. I am a loyal citizen of the DDR.'

'Then why are you no longer a member of the Free German Youth?'

Alex was lost for words. A pregnant silence hung in the air.

'You may go.' The younger man paused as he glanced at his file. 'Master Ostermann, we will call you again if we require any further assistance.'

Alex got up to leave and was surprised his legs could still carry him out of the room.

CHAPTER 7

A week after his trip into West Germany, Unterleutnant Kohl was called into the office of his senior officer, Colonel Theissen. 'We have bad news on the Hannover operation,' he told him. 'There have been arrests. A man and a woman shot dead. Our contacts with the Red Army Faction are convinced you betrayed them. It's too much like the Munich operation. They think you're the kiss of death.'

Kohl framed his response with care. Theissen could have him down in the basement steaming open envelopes for the rest of his career.

'Colonel, I can assure you I followed procedures exactly as instructed,' said Kohl. 'These people are complete bunglers.'

'I'm sure you did. And I'm sure they are,' said Theissen plainly. 'But we shall take you off Western operations for now. Wait until everything settles down.'

Kohl was disappointed. He would miss the chance to buy the goods he liked and the ones that fetched such a good price in the East. The perks far outweighed the dangers of trips like those.

'You can go back to domestic work for a while,' said Theissen, and handed him a file. 'Put in some time with Sektion 20. These two are in need of attention. I'm sure you're just the man to sort them out.'

Sektion 20 dealt with dissidents. Kohl was sent for a short session of retraining. He was instructed on how young people, infected by Western culture, were the greatest threat to the Republik. 'Adversarial asocials', 'negative-decadents' was how the directives described them. Kohl didn't need to be told this. He knew exactly what they were talking about.

Geli and Alex Ostermann fitted that profile snugly, spreading the ideology of the enemy with their music and personal appearance. They were prime candidates for preventative hindrance – no question about it. The boy was transparently under the influence of the class enemy and in thrall to the capitalist lifestyle. And he was an associate of a known border violator. She had had close relationships with adversarial asocials in the past. And now her coursework at college was displaying harmful tendencies.

It was important, Kohl realised, to make a good job of this assignment. His actions in Hannover had been criti- cised. The Red Army Faction had made it plain they considered him a class enemy and that relations with the Stasi were now extremely strained. Herr Kohl knew he was under suspicion. He had to prove he was one of them.

Kohl had re-read his Stasi training documents – especially the *Dictionary of Political Operative Work*. It was not enough to merely monitor and chastise asocials like the Ostermann brats; the instruction manual put great store in reforming them – or, as the instruction manual had it, 'shaking and changing the perspectives of oppositional negative elements and even forcing a differentiated, political-ideological recovery'.

That would be the desired outcome in this case. The Ostermann children seemed lost to the Party, but they came from good stock and their parents' loyalty had never been questioned. Kohl decided he would pull out all the stops and do whatever he could to bring them back to the straight and narrow path of the Party.

He inserted a blank sheet of paper into his typewriter and began to peck at the keys with his index fingers.

```
Operational transaction
• Container to be opened on Geli
Ostermann with immediate effect.
• Container to be opened on Alex
Ostermann with immediate effect.
• Request VSH index cards to be created
for operationally substantive information
on aforementioned subjects. Institute for
Technical Investigations to be informed
and radio counter-surveillance and
clothing and vehicle technology prepared.
```

• Variable base B 1000 Swallow to be made available for surveillance.

• Incriminating materials and visual and aural evidence to be collected.

• Specialists to carry out non-violent conspirative opening of Ostermann household to facilitate inspection and fulfilment of task.

• Key to be obtained via school search for reprehensible literature. All bags to be checked and suspect keys copied.

CC: ZAIG Central Evaluation
 Dept.14 Detention
 Dept.M Postal Surveillance
 Directorate 7 Observation
 ZKG Illegal Emigration
 Dept.26 Telephone Surveillance

CHAPTER 8

Alex took a deep breath and knocked on the door of Sophie's apartment. He'd only seen her once or twice since they'd walked home from school with Geli. Everyone knew about Holger at school. Maybe she was anxious about being friends with someone who was so closely associated with a 'border violator'. Then Alex had begun to worry that she'd asked him out to annoy her parents. He really liked Sophie, and hoped she wasn't toying with him, but didn't want to meet her parents.

The first thing Alex noticed when he approached her fifth floor apartment was the mat outside the door. It was red, with a black outline of the interlocking handshake that was the centre symbol of the SED party logo.

Sophie answered the door and gave him such a big smile his anxiety vanished in an instant. She ushered him in to the living room where her parents were standing by the window, Frau Kirsch with hands clasped tightly before her, Herr Kirsch with hands behind his back.

A wall-hanging celebrating the industrial achievements

of East Germany sat above the fireplace and even the tray on which Frau Kirsch brought the coffee and cakes had a marquetry inlay of electric locomotives and chemistry works above the DDR's flag. On the mantelpiece were ornaments of Lenin and the Red Flag. Alex wondered if Herr and Frau Kirsch had a bedspread with Lenin on it and tried not to laugh.

'And what do you want to do in life?' said Herr Kirsch, who was wondering what Alex was smirking at.

'I think I shall follow my mother into teaching,' he said. 'Perhaps music, perhaps German, I can't decide. I go to a school in Schöneweide for my work experience.' Everyone in his year at school had to go one day a week. Most of his fellow students had been sent to power stations or factories. Alex had landed a cushy number in a school two stops down on the train. He enjoyed it though. He was a good teacher and the younger kids all liked him.

'Well, you need to make up your mind soon. And you will have to have a haircut if you are to be accepted into higher education.'

The conversation flagged. Herr Kirsch asked if Alex was keen on sport. He wasn't. What had he done recently with the Free German Youth? He wasn't a member. Had he heard General Secretary Honecker's recent speech on the importance of factor utilisation on economic growth? He hadn't.

Sophie drank her coffee so fast it scalded her throat

and announced they were going to be late for the party.

'But it's about to rain, *Mein Schätzchen*,' said her mother.

'I have a headache,' Sophie said. 'I need some fresh air.'

'How d'you think that went?' asked Alex as they walked to the tram stop.

Sophie sniggered. 'Marvellous.' Then she paused and said, 'It could have been worse. They let me go, didn't they?' She hooked her arm round his. 'I think they think you're all right.' She didn't sound very convincing. Then she perked up. 'I told them you were friends with Lili Weber. That impressed them, at least! She's a fine role model for East German youth.'

She leaned closer and whispered, 'Have you heard any more about Holger?'

'It doesn't sound good,' he said. 'Holger's sister told me they've been going to the police station every day to try to find out what's happened to him. Now they're being told they'll be prosecuted for slandering the State if they carry on making a fuss. Holger's sister says they don't know whether he escaped or is in prison somewhere. No one will tell them.'

'Let's hope they find out soon,' said Sophie. 'It must be horrible not knowing.' They both shrugged. There was nothing more to say.

Their tram took them down Karl-Marx-Allee. Looking out of the window at the shops, cafés and workers' apartments, all built after the war, Alex thought its creators had lost the plot. The buildings were too hefty and the avenue too wide and empty.

Sophie instinctively shared his thoughts. 'I always feel like an ant down here.'

The tram trundled towards Alexanderplatz and the TV Tower. They got off to walk to the café bar where the party was being held. Alex shivered in the dark winter night. He was glad he had brought his pullover – the black one his mother had knitted for his birthday.

Away from the grand architecture of Karl-Marx-Allee and Alexanderplatz the buildings looked more dilapidated. Many were caked with soot or had cracked plaster peeling away to reveal the brick and timber beneath. Three cars sat in an almost empty car park – huddled together as if for protection or company. Two were ubiquitous Trabis, the other a black sedan from before the war. Alex looked at its lovely curves and sleek aerodynamic design and wondered why they didn't make cars as beautiful as that any more.

Alex and Sophie passed a tall, distinguished-looking man who was busy cleaning the street with a sturdy wicker broom. When he saw Alex, he looked away. It was only when they were some way down the road that Alex realised the man was Geli's old photography tutor, Herr Lang.

The venue was called Café Wolfgang and you reached it by climbing a flight of stairs above a furniture shop to a large first-floor room. Several of their friends were already there, sitting in the corner with Emmy, the birthday girl. The plan was to have a meal and then a dance.

The waiter looked very dapper with a smart black suit and blue spotted bow tie. Alex wondered why he'd bothered. Perhaps he was trying to make up for the rest of the café. It was so dreary. Shabby carpet, wallpaper that hadn't been changed since 1950, and a bar counter that was so worn the pattern had faded to a grey scuzz.

Emmy's friends were OK but there was too much talk of the Free German Youth for Alex's liking.

They were about to order a meal when Nadel arrived with Beate, another girl from their class. Alex didn't like Nadel and noticed at once he was wearing the green and yellow enamel badge of the Free German Youth group leaders on his jacket. Much to Alex's discomfort they sat immediately opposite him and Sophie.

Beate was wearing a polyester fabric design that was everywhere that winter – a violent zigzag pattern, like a regular longitudinal wave on an oscilloscope, in bright reds and blues. Everything from trouser suits to mini, midi and maxi skirts were made out of that material. Beate had made a pair of trousers and a matching waistcoat from hers. She and Sophie fell into conversation about the difficulties of making your own clothes, leaving Alex and Nadel to make polite conversation.

They were all drinking bottles of *Radeberger* Pilsner. By the time the *Jägerschnitzels* and noodles arrived they were getting rowdy.

Nadel was singing the praises of the Trabi, and saying how it was a better car than the West German equivalent, the Volkswagen Beetle. Alex wasn't so sure.

'The Beetle is tainted by its Nazi past,' said Nadel loftily. It had originally been designed for the Nazi 'Strength Through Joy' organisation, as Hitler's 'people's car'.

'Yes, it was cheap and mass produced,' said Alex, who knew all this, 'just like the Trabi. The Volkswagen goes faster,' Alex continued. 'A whole 30 kph faster.'

'And how do you know that?' said Nadel.

'Come on,' laughed Alex. 'Don't tell me you never watch the West German TV? It's there in the adverts – a top speed of 130 kph.'

'I don't pollute my brain with dross from the West,' said Nadel.

'Too bad. You might learn something useful,' said Alex. Sophie kicked him under the table. But Alex would not let it go.

'And you can get Beetles in all sorts of colours – red, gold, black, white, whatever,' he said. 'What colours d'you get with a Trabi?' Alex held up his hand to count. 'Blue . . .' He held up one finger. 'Green . . .' Two fingers. 'Er . . . ? No. That's it.'

'Different colours are a waste of workers' time and a sign of bourgeois decadence,' said Nadel. He was getting flustered. Everyone had stopped to listen.

'Go on, admit it.' Alex was sensing victory. 'You see

Beetles all over the world. If you ever watched the British or American films on Western TV, you'd see Beetles on the streets of London and Los Angeles. I have never seen a Trabi anywhere outside of the Eastern Countries.'

Nadel had no answer to that. Alex moved in for the kill. 'Maybe the fact that the Trabi has no fuel gauge puts people in the West off buying it?' he said with a smirk.

'You just need to keep an eye on your kilometres and remember how much fuel you have put in,' said Nadel. 'It's no problem for anyone with a brain in their head.'

'A fuel gauge seemed such an obvious piece of equipment on a car . . .'

Nadel huffed impatiently. 'The simpler the car, the less chance of a breakdown.'

'I've seen our Trabi engine being repaired on the kitchen table enough times to know that's not the case,' said Alex.

The others round the table all laughed at that.

Nadel had had enough. 'That is simply not true,' he declared with frightening certainty. 'The Trabi is more reliable and cheaper. What could be a better advert for socialism?'

'Advert?' said Alex. 'Bit of a capitalist word, isn't it?'

'Alex . . .' Nadel leaned back on his chair and replied with magisterial condescension, 'your frivolity will be the end of you.' Alex reached his foot under the table and pulled the back leg of Nadel's chair towards him. Nadel

61

crashed to the floor and his beer toppled after him, covering his head and shoulders. Dripping and humiliated, he scrambled to his feet and launched himself at Alex in a blind fury.

Alex was no fighter. The last time he had come to blows with anyone was in kindergarten. He held up his arms to fend off the blows and waited for the other lads in the party to pull Nadel off him.

A tirade of obscenities followed before Nadel hurried to the lavatory to wash the beer from his hair. The waiter came over to Emmy and whispered in her ear.

'You horrible boy,' she cried. 'Ruining my party. And now we've been asked to leave.'

Alex suddenly felt less triumphant. 'I'm sorry, Emmy. I'll talk to the waiter. I shall go.'

Sophie was looking at him with open exasperation. Alex knew there were others there who lived close by them. She would not have to travel home alone.

He spoke to the waiter, apologised for the trouble and left.

Alex was so hot and bothered and angry with himself for spoiling the evening that he was halfway to the tram stop in Alexanderplatz when a chill gust of wind blew straight through him and he realised he had left his pullover behind. It wasn't just the cold that made him go back for it. His mother had made it for him with the best wool she could afford. She would be very upset if he lost it.

When he returned, most of the diners at Café Wolfgang had abandoned their tables for the dance floor. They were moving fairly listlessly to some home-grown pop song Alex half recognised from the radio. In the tradition of East German discos, the song was taken off after a few bars and the introduction to 'Get It On' by the British group T. Rex energised the dance floor like a jolt of electricity. Alex smiled at the stupid rule that demanded two-thirds of recorded music played in public places had to come from communist countries. Most venues got round it by playing brief snippets of their own music and Western songs in their entirety.

He picked up his pullover and looked around for Sophie to tell her he was sorry, but he couldn't see her. Now he had calmed down he was starting to feel embarrassed about his behaviour. He hurried down the stairs but as he came out into Greifswalder Strasse, Alex heard some movement behind him. He peered up the dimly lit stairs to see two figures having a heated exchange. 'Get away from me.' Alex recognised her voice at once.

Looking again he could see Sophie trying to break away, but the man with her was holding on to her arm. Alex ran up the stairs. 'Hey,' he said to the man. 'Let her go.'

The fellow was older and stronger than Alex. Without saying a word he turned and shoved Alex off his feet. Sophie broke free and grabbed Alex's arm just as he was about to fall down the stairs. They took off together, leaving the man to hurl insults at them both, but at least he didn't follow them.

'That was Charlie,' she said. 'I went out with him a couple of times when I first arrived here. I think he followed me here. I told him to leave me alone weeks ago. When he realised I wasn't joking, he didn't say much, but he had this stubborn determined look on his face. I knew that wouldn't be the end of it.

'And Mutter and Vater thought he was just right for me,' she said indignantly. 'Youth group leader. Exemplary socialist youth. Complete creep would be more like it.'

They had barely gone twenty metres when she hooked a hand round his elbow and they walked together arm in arm.

'Am I forgiven?' he said. 'I'm sorry I was an idiot with Nadel. He gets up my nose.'

'You were doing so well,' said Sophie and pulled him closer to her, 'until the business with the chair.' She suppressed a chuckle. 'That wasn't strictly necessary.'

Her mood changed abruptly. 'Charlie,' she spat. 'He came on to me here, then when I decided to go home, he insisted he would run me back on his moped. Then he grabbed me and tried to kiss me.'

Alex decided it was the moment to be bold.

'What, like this?' he said, and turned and kissed her.

She was soft and warm and still tasted of the raspberry liquor he'd bought her just before the evening all went wrong.

'Exactly like that,' she said.

After they kissed again, and she rested her head on his shoulder.

'I started to worry about you going home on your own,' Alex said.

'I'm glad you came back,' she said.

If they walked home rather than take the tram, they decided, they would have just enough money for another drink. So they went to Café Luxembourg on Karl-Marx-Allee and had another beer and raspberry liquor.

It was a long walk back to Treptower, but Alex thought it was one of the best nights of his life.

CHAPTER 9

Sophie asked Alex to meet her in the park after school on Saturday afternoon. They huddled together against the cold and walked down to the funfair. She carried a bag on her shoulder and wouldn't tell Alex what was in it. 'Only after you buy me a coffee,' she smiled.

They enjoyed themselves at the fair, riding on the mechanical swans and the donkeys, even though they felt far too old for them. It was fun until Alex noticed a middle-aged man hovering in the background wherever they went. 'I saw him when we came out of your apartment,' he said. 'And he's still hanging round now.'

Sophie looked over and couldn't see him. 'Look, he's turned his back on us now. He's buying something from the *Currywurst* stall,' said Alex.

She laughed. 'Probably an old pervert. Gets his thrills from following young couples about. Forget about him.'

They walked home soon afterwards. As they reached the entrance to her apartment she handed over a square package wrapped in brown paper.

'Don't let anyone see it,' she whispered. 'Grandma brought it back from West Berlin. It's definitely not music the Party would approve of. I wouldn't dream of playing it in the house if my parents were around.'

'What is it?' asked Alex.

'You'll see!'

Alex felt hard cardboard through the brown paper. His eyes lit up. 'You have the sleeve too?' he asked.

'Yes. Grandma got it through no problem. This one has no picture of the group on it. And no title too. There's no writing on the cover at all. The guards thought it looked harmless.'

It was the records where the group on the cover had really long hair and wore hippy clothes that vexed the border guards.

'How much did she pay?'

'A couple of Marks. I tell her what to look for and she gets them from second-hand stalls.'

Alex was doubly curious now. He had rarely seen a Western rock album in its sleeve. Forbidden music usually came in a plain paper inner sleeve with just the vinyl record to tell you what it was. No details. Nothing to give it away.

'Be careful who hears it, Alex.'

When Alex went to bed that night, he wedged the waste paper bin against the door. Carefully removing the square package from under his bed, he gingerly slipped the record out to study it under the glare of his reading lamp.

Alex was puzzled by the cover. It looked like a folk

music album. As Sophie had said, it had no lettering, just a small, framed oil painting of an old man with a bundle of sticks on his back that was hanging on a wall with peeling wallpaper. You could open the cover out like a book and on the back you could see the wall belonged to a partly demolished house. Beyond lay wasteland and wintry sky, and a tower block as bleak as anything in East Berlin.

On the grey inner sleeve were strange rune-like symbols which whispered of the occult. That made sense to Alex. What he held was forbidden knowledge. Then there was a list of titles. 'Black Dog', 'Rock and Roll' – words he recognised.

Alex scrutinised the sparse information for meaning. Headley Grange, Hampshire. Island Studios, London. Sunset Sound, Los Angeles. Were these places where the record was made? He pictured these forbidden cities, imagining sun-drenched streets with people who dressed how they liked and wore their hair as long they wanted.

On the label of the vinyl record he saw the words Led Zeppelin. They were his favourite group. He loved how they could be 'heavy' on one song, and light and airy on the next. Alex had heard they had travelled all over the world – apart from the communist countries. He couldn't imagine anything more wonderful than being their guitarist, Jimmy Page. And he bet Jimmy lived somewhere where you didn't have to lug coal up six flights of stairs and have a shower in a tub in the kitchen.

As he slid the disc back into the sleeve he felt something else inside. It was a colour photograph snipped from a magazine of two men on a stage – curling towards each other like circling cats. One had a mass of blond ringlets and although he wore a girl's floral blouse he reminded Alex of a Viking marauder. That must be the singer, Robert Plant. The other carried a Les Paul guitar slung low on his hips. He was rake thin, had a great mop of dark wavy hair and a matador jacket embroidered with red poppies. So that was what Jimmy Page looked like! If both of them appeared in East Berlin, they would have been attacked on the street.

A record like this could fetch two hundred Marks on the black market – four or five months' rent. And he was going to hear it for nothing! But he'd have to wait until his parents were out. And he would use their new headphones. These were difficult to get hold of but Frank knew the right people. Headphones meant you could listen as loud as you liked and not have to worry about the neighbours. Alex lay awake wondering what Led Zeppelin had produced this time. Then he drifted off to sleep listening to the guard dogs howling at the Wall.

The next morning both his parents went out to play football and hockey for their work teams. They were always doing something communal like that – offering their services to paint the school windows, rattling collection boxes for North Vietnam – Alex wondered how they found the time. As soon as they had left he showed his acquisition to Geli. She adored the magazine photograph. 'I'd love to work at a concert like that . . . all those lights and shapes.'

Alex was impatient to hear his record. The pop and crackle of the needle on vinyl filled his headphones with the first track, 'Black Dog'. Then came a strange clinking sound, like a machine being wound up, swiftly interrupted by the singer, then the rest of the band lumbered in with a great anaconda of a riff that snaked and slithered around in his head, the drums clanking and thudding like an old steam engine. Alex could not understand how men wearing women's blouses could make music that lurched and juddered like a prehistoric beast in heat.

Geli and Alex spent the rest of the morning listening again and again, enthralled. Alex wondered what it would be like to walk the streets of London, Los Angeles, and even Headley Grange, Hampshire, wherever that was.

CHAPTER 10

On his way to school on Monday morning, Alex waited at the corner of the park for Sophie. He felt the crisp cold in his throat and watched his breath curl away in the bright winter sunshine. He couldn't believe his luck. A lovely girl. Fantastic music. It was a potent combination.

She came running up to him and he held open his arms to hug her. Checking they were out of anyone's earshot, Alex said, 'Led Zeppelin! Wow!! Just brilliant!!! Does your grandma often get you records?'

'Big secret,' she said.

Then she decided to tell him. 'She's done it a few times. I tell her what to look for. Usually she'll slip it inside the sleeve of something innocuous, like Tom Jones or Bert Kaempfert. But she didn't need to with this one.

'You hold on to it. Keep it as long as you like. I play it every time my parents go out. I need to give it a rest.'

Alex told her he was going to call his group Black Dog after the first song on the record.

'So you're still going to play, without Holger?' said Sophie.

'Suppose so,' said Alex. 'I don't see why we should stop.'

Sophie told him her parents thought she only listened to classical music. But she was sure they would disapprove if they knew the truth. Alex could sympathise. His parents hadn't banned him from listening to Western rock music, but they made it plain they didn't like it.

His dad was funny like that. 'Ach, do what you must,' he would say when he and Geli put some forbidden rock music on the family record player. 'We are not the Gestapo. But play it quietly. I don't want the neighbours to complain.' Sometimes, when it was too 'heavy', like that Black Sabbath record they'd borrowed, he asked them to take it off. They had an instinct for what the Party would and would not tolerate.

'Hey, by the way, Mutter and Vater have asked if you would come for tea next Sunday,' said Alex. 'Do you mind?'

She smiled. 'Of course not.'

Frank and Gretchen were keen to meet Sophie. They knew her parents from Party meetings and had seen her around the school. They thought she was a good match for their Alex. And knowing people like the Kirschs would certainly be useful.

Over in Normannenstrasse, another item of evidence arrived for Alex Ostermann's container.

Subject continues to make openly hostile comparisons of DDR and Federal Republic,

displaying delusional bourgeois
aspirations. False consciousness
undoubtedly further corrupted by Western
broadcasts which he openly admits to
observing. Concern expressed regarding
potentially negative influence on Sophie
Kirsch, daughter of Arnd and Katherina
Kirsch, whose loyalty to DDR is beyond
question. Recommend close monitoring.

The week passed quickly and on Friday evening, as they walked home from school, Alex asked Sophie if they could hook up, just the two of them, before she came round to meet his parents.

Sunday itself was a damp, cold day. Alex and Sophie shivered as they trudged through the drifts of dead leaves in the park and hoped the rain would hold off.

'How's the band going?' she asked

'We're playing again next Thursday,' said Alex. 'I don't think we'll look for another guitarist. It would be disloyal. And I still haven't heard anything more about Holger.'

'Maybe he got away?' said Sophie.

Alex took his courage in his hands and asked her an awkward question. He knew the answer would have a direct effect on what he thought about her.

'What do you think about what the school says – that he's a traitor for going?'

She thought hard before she answered. 'Mutter and

Vater would say he was. He's been looked after by the State. He's been educated by the State and he should stay here to help build a good future for us all.'

Alex wished he hadn't asked. Then she leaned closer to him and whispered, 'But I think he was brave to try to get away . . .'

'Me too,' said Alex. But he wasn't going to say any more. What they were saying was treason. He was keen to change the subject. He started to tell her about his group. Sophie's eyes glazed over. Alex recognised her expression. It was the one he put on in politics classes when he was pretending to be interested. And now it was starting to rain.

'Enough about groups,' she said with a steely look. 'Let's go in here.' She steered him towards a church on the edge of the park.

Alex liked churches. They were a peaceful oasis in the busy city.

They went inside the deserted building and sat at the back of the nave. 'You don't go to church, do you?' he asked.

'God, no,' she said. 'My parents would have a heart attack! They think going to church is as bad as having long hair!'

Alex nodded. He started to imitate his father. '"No child of ours is going to be brainwashed with religious dogma." But they listen to Bach and Handel at home – the religious stuff, with choirs and all.

'I think it's stupid,' continued Alex. 'So what if you go to church occasionally. I like to sit in the silence and look at the stained-glass windows.'

'Sometimes there's a choir rehearsal,' said Sophie. 'I listen outside. It's beautiful music, isn't it?'

'We should go together, sneak in at the back one day,' said Alex and squeezed her hand.

'Mutter and Vater would kill me,' she said.

Alex was beginning to shiver. 'Come on, it's getting cold.' They walked home in the drizzle. 'Mutti's cooking a joint of pork in your honour.'

Arriving at the apartment it was wonderful to walk into the fug of the Ostermanns' warm living room with its steamed-up windows and the delicious aroma of roast pork. Alex's family greeted Sophie warmly and Gretchen took their damp coats to dry in front of the coal fire.

Sophie noticed at once the photographs Alex's parents had placed on the mantelpiece. 'Don't they look sweet,' she said. Gretchen beamed with pride. Alex particularly hated the picture of himself and Geli in their Young Pioneers outfits – both of them in an identical white nylon shirt and matching little blue neckerchief. It was a constant embarrassment when friends came to visit.

Alex wondered if that had been the last time his parents had truly felt proud of them. They were ten or eleven there. Geli was still taller than him then, and he was looking up to her with obvious affection.

When he was that age, he had really believed

everything the SED told him. That the people of the DDR were all working together to build a workers' paradise and by the time he was a grown man their country would be the envy of the world. It was like believing in the Easter Bunny or Santa Claus.

'Dinner's ready,' shouted Frank, and asked Geli to open a bottle of Bulgarian wine he'd found in the grocer's that morning.

Round the table, talk turned to fashion.

'Are those Levi's jeans?' Sophie asked Geli.

'Yes, my boyfriend gave them to me.'

'It must be love,' said Sophie.

Alex was slightly ashamed of his own jeans. The East German Boxer brand were made of polyester rather than cotton, the stitching was all over the place, and they never fitted quite right or faded in the wash like real Levi's. But a pair of Levi's would cost a week's wages and there was no way his mother and father would agree to that.

So many clothes in the shops were exactly the same, and you had to make your own adjustments if you wanted to look different. Alex knew Sophie was handy with a sewing machine, rattling away on it to alter the fit or adding different buttons. Some of the youth group leaders and teachers disapproved. Wanting to be different was a bourgeois failing – 'Western egotism'.

Gretchen said, 'Ten years ago you could get arrested for wearing jeans. Too much a symbol of the class enemy

– the United States! But even the Stasi have come to realise it's just fashion, not a political protest.'

'It's like the pop music, or the rock music, whatever it's called,' said Frank. 'Ten years ago you could get beaten up for listening to it – even be given hard labour! But we've moved on there too. We're even producing our own pop groups now. I heard the Puhdys went to play in America!'

Alex felt like saying the Puhdys were insipid crap, but he didn't want a scene on Sophie's first visit. Besides, his parents were doing their best to show what open-minded and forward-thinking socialists they were.

Geli asked Sophie about her red blouse. 'I found it in a second-hand clothes shop.'

'Is it real cotton?' Geli could hardly contain her admiration. Sophie nodded.

'I don't get on with *Präsent 20*,' said Geli. Almost everything people wore in East Germany was made of man-made fibre. *Präsent 20* was the latest one. It had been unveiled at the twentieth anniversary celebrations for the East German state and hailed as the Party's 'gift to the people'.

'But it's so easy to wash,' said Gretchen, 'and it never shrinks.'

'It's sticky,' said Geli, 'and if you go to a dance, half an hour in it's glued to you with sweat.'

Sophie agreed. 'I always get cotton if I can find it in second-hand stores. I wish it wasn't so expensive to buy it new. I can't afford to shop in *Exquisit*. I do a lot of rummaging through second-hand clothes!'

Frank was looking uneasy. 'I know everything's a year or two behind what's fashionable in the West,' he said, 'but most people don't mind. The ordinary workers – they just want hard-wearing clothes that are easy to take care of. Like those made of *Präsent 20*.'

'Come on, Vati, that's ridiculous and you know it,' said Geli. 'The government decides what people should wear and sends instructions to the *Mode-Institut* in Berlin. A group of stuffy old *Onkels* decides what is fashionable here!'

An awkward silence followed. 'So where did you go this afternoon?' Gretchen asked Sophie, changing the subject.

'We went for a walk in the park and then sat in the church on Köpenicker Landstrasse,' she blurted out unthinkingly. The strong red wine had gone to her head.

Frank and Gretchen looked alarmed. Sophie realised she had said the wrong thing at once and blushed.

'Well, it was raining,' Alex said. 'There's no harm in going in, is there?'

'Alex. All that hair on your head is clouding your thinking,' said Frank. 'Maybe your brain is overheating. Church services – who goes to them?'

'Christians,' said Alex.

'And who else?'

Alex was at a loss.

'You know the churches are a magnet for malcontents in our society. And who do you always see outside a church on Sundays, taking photographs and keeping a note of who is coming in and going out?'

Alex nodded his head. They didn't need to say any more.

Alex walked Sophie home. 'I'm sorry I mentioned the church,' she said. 'I can't make out your Mutter and Vater. They're quite different from mine. You know exactly where you are with mine. You aren't allowed to say anything bad about the DDR. Your parents seem a bit more open-minded. But then you say something and you feel you've really overstepped the mark.'

'Sometimes I don't understand them either,' said Alex. He kissed her on the forehead. 'Don't worry about the church. Besides, Vati is right. Who wants the Stasi taking pictures of you? There's no sense in inviting trouble.'

Alex returned home to a strained atmosphere. It had all started so well. And he really wanted them to like Sophie.

'She's a lovely girl,' said his mother. 'But she has some surprisingly relaxed views for the child of such strict Party members.'

His dad was still annoyed with him. 'You in your invincible youth! You think nothing can touch you and nothing can go wrong. I think you should have a haircut.' He always said that after they'd had any sort of disagreement about politics.

Alex grew exasperated. His hair was hardly long – not

like the pictures of the hippies and freaks you saw on the pop programmes on West German television.

'Hansi at school has hair just as long as mine,' said Alex.

'Hansi at school is a prize athlete, a squad leader in the Free German Youth and he gets top marks in his political theory essays. You do none of these things.'

Frank ruffled his son's hair and tried to sound affable. 'It's easier now for you longhairs. When Mutti and I were young, with the Beat groups becoming popular, you could be chased by the police and put in prison if you looked like you do.'

Alex let out an exasperated sigh.

'What do you really think, Vati?' he said. 'I never know with you or Mutti. Is it just a big game of doing the right thing?'

Frank looked irritated, but tried to control his temper. 'Your mother and I live in the real world,' he said tersely. 'We admire the Party, we admire Comrade Honecker, and we believe in our government and country. It is not perfect, but it's what we've got, and it is easy to criticise, especially if you spend half your time watching West German television. We know the rules. And we know what you and Geli need to do to get on.'

'You are a bright boy,' said Gretchen. 'You have the opportunity to do something magnificent with your life, for our country and for yourself. Or you can carry on like this. You worry us, Alex. They will see you as a layabout

80

and a troublemaker and you'll be lucky if you get a job as a dustman.'

'We remember what it was like after the war,' said Frank. 'Your mother and I, we were nine, ten. We were starving. There was nowhere to live. Hitler had destroyed our country. Now look at us. We have a fine place to live, we have food, we even have a washing machine and a colour television. Everyone has a job. That's progress. I believe in that.'

'But they have all these things in West Germany too,' said Alex, careful to sound reasonable rather than provocative.

'Yes, but they have no care for each other. If you turn up late for work, you are sacked immediately. Thousands of people are thrown out of work when the capitalists are not making their precious profit. Rents are extortionate. There is no free childcare, no free nurseries, they only think about themselves. It is a selfish place, Alex. People do not look after each other. And the industrialists, the politicians, the council leaders, they are all former Nazis. It makes my flesh creep to think that the old men running the West have all spent their early years strutting around in Nazi uniforms *Sieg Heil*ing with the worst of them. Here in the East, at least, we have purged and punished our Nazis. I would not want to live over there.'

Alex was getting more and more wound up. 'Wouldn't you like to go out of the house and not have to remember to take a carrier bag with you – in case you saw something in the shops you hadn't seen for six months? Wouldn't you like to be able to buy fresh fruit and vegetables whenever you wanted instead of making do with jars of pickled stuff?'

Alex had had enough. He was tired and he wanted to go to bed. He knew his friend Anton would have been beaten black and blue by now if he'd argued with his father like this.

'I'll stay clear of churches when there's a service on, Vati. I promise.'

Frank watched his son leave the room with a sinking heart. Alex was in his final year at school now, and his future was uncertain. Only a few of Alex's year group would be going on to higher education – and they all knew that this had only a little to do with their ability. It was mainly down to how loyal their family was to the State. Geli had managed to get into the *Erweiterte Oberschule* – Extended Secondary School – thanks to Frank and Gretchen's impeccable Party record and her own academic excellence, but things were looking doubtful for Alex.

He didn't have the fear – the stomach-tightening chill of falling foul of the regime – that was always there in the background. Frank and Gretchen knew. Alex and Geli had yet to learn. Especially Alex.

CHAPTER 11

Alex sniffed the air during the morning break and decided that today was the first day of spring. There was a warmth to the sunshine and you could imagine the crocuses coming up and buds appearing on the trees. Spring usually filled him with hope and energy, but today he found it hard to summon either. Last night he had been to visit Holger's apartment. His mother ushered him in swiftly and immediately scolded him for coming to see them. But she made such a half-hearted job of it that Alex could tell she was glad he was there.

'Look at this,' said Frau Vogel and thrust a document at him. It was a statement from the State Bank. 'We opened a savings account for Holger on his sixteenth birthday. Now it has been closed and they've sent us this.'

The word 'Deceased' had been stamped across it.

'I went to the bank and asked if we could withdraw the money,' she said, her voice rising in exasperation. 'They said only the account holder could authorise a withdrawal.'

'But it says he's died,' said Alex, who wondered why she wasn't more upset. He was beginning to feeling increasingly bewildered.

'He's not dead,' said Frau Vogel. 'I'm his mother. I'd know. I'd feel it in my bones. They're just playing with us. I don't care about the money, it's only a few hundred Marks. I'd just like to know what's happened. He's either in prison here, or he's escaped to the West. They're just not going to tell us. I know they're bastards, but I can't believe they wouldn't tell us if he'd been killed.'

Alex left soon afterwards, asking her to promise to tell him if she heard anything. He lay awake that night and thought about how awful it must be for Frau Vogel – when every knock at the door or postal delivery might bring faint hope of news of her son. His sadness was soon eclipsed by anger. He had a terrible feeling that Holger had been shot dead. A sixteen-year-old boy, in cold blood. No wonder they wanted to keep that quiet.

It was Dr Richard Sorge Day at the school. Sorge, the celebrated German-Soviet spy who had been stationed in Japan during the war, was a national hero. Stamps, post-cards, school textbooks were all devoted to his exploits. The Young Pioneers crowded on to the assembly hall stage in their white and blue uniforms and sang songs about him under the slogan *Dr Richard Sorge, Unser Vorbild* – Dr Richard Sorge, Our Model.

That afternoon the sun was still shining and Alex was keen to get to the park with Sophie. But first he had to sit through double politics. Herr Würfel was telling them the Socialist Unity Party was the conscience and organiser of the German working class.

Sometimes Alex could not even pretend to be interested. Würfel pointed a stick at a stupefyingly dull diagram showing the various hierarchies within the Party.

'As the child is to the parent, so the citizen is to the State. The Party represents everything that is true in society and the political system.'

Alex could feel himself falling asleep. He was beginning to loathe school and tried to remember when he'd last been interested in a lesson.

Würfel threw his chalk at Alex. It hit him square on the top of his head. He jerked upright, instantly awake. 'I am sure Dr Richard Sorge never nodded off in politics lessons,' announced Würfel. The class snickered.

Würfel sent Alex off with a copy of *Economic Legislation for Socialism* and told him he expected a précis of the first three chapters on his desk first thing the next morning.

At breaktime Alex and Sophie sat together in the school yard, away from the others. Even then, they whispered. Just the other day a rumour had gone round that the perimeter of the playing field was bugged with Stasi microphones and it was only safe to talk if you sat in the middle of the field rather than at the edge. The school was planning an anniversary celebration of the birth of the Socialist Unity Party and he was wondering how he could get away with doing as little as possible for this event.

Alex loathed parades. 'The last one, we had to carry great big pictures of the Party leaders. It was surreal. I had to carry Honecker. His picture was much bigger than all the others, in case we forgot he was the leader!'

They were laughing and Sophie shushed him. 'Quiet – someone will hear.'

Alex said, 'Come to the fair with me tonight. Geli is going to meet Lili there too. We could meet up early. Have a *Currywurst* and a beer. Even go on the Ferris wheel.' The fair was at the far end of Treptower Park – a brisk twenty-minute walk from their apartments.

'Lili's a bit frightening, isn't she,' said Sophie.

'She's all right. Geli and I have known her for years. Please come along.'

Alex admired anyone who could do well at sport. His entire childhood had been blighted by early morning athletics competitions – freezing to death on a bleak football pitch, waiting for the winter sun to come up while the school tannoy blared out the national anthem or brisk brass-band music.

That afternoon their routine was interrupted by the Stasi. They descended on the school when Alex's year was out playing hockey and football. When they returned to shower and collect their bags, they were barred from entry to the changing rooms. A Ministry of State Security guard stood by the doors to both the male and female changing rooms. No explanation was given.

Ten minutes later they saw three plain-clothes Stasi leave the building.

'They looked like creeps – especially the big one with the lank greasy hair,' Alex muttered to Anton as they were allowed back in.

The whole year was called into the school assembly hall. Herr Roth, the Principal, announced that the Ministry of State Security had visited for routine checks and the school had been given a clean bill of health. As the kids walked home, the usual rumours went round about the Stasi looking for Western newspaper cuttings, pornography, drugs . . . Alex laughed at that one. They were told that young people in the West took lots of drugs. Alex hadn't seen anything like it in East Berlin. The nearest he got to drugs was sharing a cigarette with Anton. He didn't like to admit it but cigarettes always made him feel a bit sick.

It had taken three minutes for Unterleutnant Erich Kohl to identify Alex Ostermann's possessions among the untidy piles of clothes and bags. He quickly located his keys in his pocket and made putty casts of them. They were never exact, these casts, but a skilled operative with a file could make minor adjustments to keys on the job.

Kohl enjoyed his work. Things had certainly moved on from the early days. The toys they gave you to play with! He had a microphone disguised as a tiepin that connected to a tiny tape recorder in his jacket. Science fiction thirty years ago! Back then, you had great big metal wheels of tape, and the hiss and crackle on them was horrendous. Kohl also loved the little cameras they had – ones that nestled in bags or lapels, which you operated with a little push button in your pocket. And the TV surveillance equipment was fantastic – stuff that looked like it had come from a laboratory or the Soviet Space Centre in Kazakhstan. Nowadays you could even record people's misdemeanours on videotape.

Although he missed his work in the Foreign Section, he had settled into the Internal Service now. Sektion 20 was performing a valuable duty – weeding out the malcontents, trying to spot the escapers. There were still too many people trying to leave – some of them were even doctors, teachers, nurses, engineers. All of them trained and nurtured by their country, only to desert it when they were ready to do some good for their comrades. It wasn't right.

He even liked the cultural stuff, although a lot of his colleagues moaned about how tedious it was – keeping an eye on the ones who showed 'negative tendencies'. But they were the ones most likely to escape. If you had some kid with long hair and hippy clothes and weird music, then it was a safe bet they weren't going to be an A-Grade student of Marxist-Leninism and destined for a career in government. Catching them young would nip those incorrect tendencies in the bud.

Alex rattled off his extra politics assignment as soon as he got home, then headed out into the winter evening to meet Sophie in the park. He was disconcerted to hear her parents had objected to her coming out with him. But they had relented when she told them who she was going to meet. Everyone knew Lili Weber.

They drank beer and ate their *Currywurst*. Alex felt happy and a little light-headed, and the curry sauce had left a pleasant sting on his lips. Sophie rested her head on his shoulders. 'It's nice, isn't it. Just the two of us. I'm glad we came early.'

'Let's go on the wheel,' said Alex. 'Catch the last of the sunset.'

Soon they were beginning their jerky, stop-start journey to the top, as the wheel emptied and filled with passengers. As they ascended, Alex caught sight of the flashing lights of a Western airliner banking over the city as it made its approach to Tegel Airport. He thought how much he would like to be one of those passengers. He was about to say as much to Sophie but something stopped him. It seemed too frank an admission, even to say to her.

The sun had gone now and in the ebbing light of the distant sky he could see the illuminated signs of the big capitalist companies over in West Berlin – Mercedes, Axel Springer Verlag . . . In school they had been taught to despise these symbols and told horror stories of how the capitalist companies exploited the workers. Alex wondered if they were really any worse than the East German industries.

They met up with Geli, and a couple of her friends,

soon after they finished their ride. She bought them two small beers and they stood around basking in the flashing lights and the booming music. Alex felt a little distracted. He had glimpsed a familiar face over the other side of the wheel and it made him feel uneasy. Was it that fellow who had been lurking around on the day Sophie had given him the Led Zeppelin record? He was about to mention it when Geli spotted Lili and shouted over to her. She was talking to another group of friends nearby, fellow students at the sports academy by the look of them, but she immediately came to join them.

They could see at once she was in the same foul mood she'd been in when they saw her before. 'She's been training too hard,' whispered Geli. 'There's too much pressure on her. Let's be gentle with her.' She looked like a box of fireworks, ready to go up.

Geli felt especially protective towards her. Lili was one of the first kids in the school to befriend her and she wasn't going to forget that. Lili had done her best to keep in touch when she had been transferred to the sports academy. They were all proud to have a friend who was a national champion.

The others drifted off and Sophie, Alex and Geli went to sit with Lili on a bench at the edge of the fair. In a few months' time she would be competing in the Olympics at Munich. Alex asked her how the training was going. Lili needed no prompting.

'"You are ambassadors in tracksuits," says the coach.

I'm sick to death of having to be an ambassador. "In your actions, your victories, you will demonstrate to the world the superiority of the socialist system." It's hard enough trying to win a race without feeling that your performance will reflect on your entire country.'

'But it's been good for you, Lili,' said Geli, trying to make her friend feel more positive. 'Look at all the things you've got out of it. The best school, travel all over the Eastern Countries. You have such an exciting life.' She put a reassuring hand on her friend's shoulder. 'And you are the best in Berlin – maybe the entire country.'

Lili nodded and put her hand on Geli's and patted it. 'Thank you,' she said. Then she looked at her watch. 'Sheisse, I forgot to take my pill.' She took out a small silver blister pack and popped out an orange pill, knocking it back with a swig of beer.

'What's this,' said Geli with a giggle. 'You on the pill? Who's the boyfriend?'

Lili bristled. Geli shrank.

'They're vitamin supplements,' she said, trying to hide her irritation. 'My coach started me on them last year. I take four a day.' Then she looked sad. 'Boyfriend? I should be so lucky. I seem to frighten boys away these days.'

Alex was not surprised. Lili had always been a bit of a tomboy, even in kindergarten, but she had been a pretty girl. Now, well into her teens, she seemed to be getting more masculine – even the shape of her face seemed manly and she had the beginnings of a moustache on her top lip.

A gang of boys and girls went past. The toughest-looking girl stared hard at Lili. 'What's your problem?' Lili said, looking the girl in the eye. Alex shrank in his seat. There were six in this gang, and only four of them.

The girl turned round and squared up to Lily, who stood up to face her. Geli put a hand on her arm. 'Lili – they're not worth a fight.' Sophie and Alex sat there in terrified silence.

'Dyke,' muttered the girl and turned to walk away. Lili picked up an empty beer bottle, gave a scream and ran after them. The gang scattered, leaving Lili standing her ground and laughing.

Two of the park police were coming over. 'Hey, you,' shouted one of them, above the blare of the fairground music. 'Stay where you are.'

Lily let the bottle fall to the ground and shatter. Now it was their turn to run. All four of them disappeared into the bushes. Ten minutes later, they were all trying to get their breath back on the other side of the park.

'Lili, that could have turned nasty,' said Geli gently. 'What if she had hit you? You might have been hurt.'

Lili was unrepentant. 'I knew they didn't have the guts for a fight,' she said.

'You frightened us half to death,' said Sophie.

'*Na und?*' said Lili.

They all parted with sullen goodbyes.

CHAPTER 12

Alex had to get to school especially early to hand in his précis to Herr Würfel and decided to go on his bike. When he unlocked the little storeroom the Ostermanns had in the basement of their apartment block, he was irritated to discover that both tyres were flat. He had to run all the way to school and arrived five minutes late. Würfel could see he was out of breath so he forgave him. He skimmed through Alex's work, making lots of encouraging noises. 'It's good. I've always known you are one of the brightest pupils. Why can't you perform like this in class?'

Alex shrugged.

Würfel said, 'You have a lot of growing up to do, Alex Ostermann. Be quick about it before it's too late.'

Alex's band reconvened in Treptower that evening. Anton and Heinz were OK with the idea of Black Dog for their name. They didn't get the Led Zeppelin reference and Alex wasn't going to let on he had the record either. It was too risky.

It was odd sitting in the living room without Holger. Alex felt guilty about having ever wished his friend would leave his group. He missed him now. He had asked Sophie to come along and hear them, and maybe sing on some of the songs. She was a bit wary but she said she'd give it a go. She was quite fidgety and Alex could tell she didn't really want to be there. He thought he'd try out his new song. He'd got some words for it now.

'Here's how it goes,' he told the boys. 'The chords are E minor, then G, then D then back to the E.' He sang and played the chorus:

> *We're up against the Wall*
> *and heading for a fall*
> *But I'm still standing tall*
> *Up against the Wall.*

Alex felt pretty pleased with those words. Geli had helped him a bit and he had even managed to come up with rhymes in another language! He wished they did English at school instead of Russian.

'Why do we have to sing in English?' said Heinz, who didn't understand what Alex was on about. 'That'll be another black mark against us.'

'English is cool,' said Anton. 'All the good groups sing in English.'

Heinz shook his head and muttered, 'I'll never get that snare drum . . .'

Anton was behaving particularly badly that day. He had a cold and was snorting horribly instead of blowing his nose. In the breaks between songs he would take a slug from a bottle of cola and let out a long, malodorous burp. Alex had noticed he quite often behaved like this when Sophie was there. She had giggled and told Alex she thought he was quite shy around girls and maybe he thought it made him look tough. 'After all, we girls can't resist a lout. Especially one who's a bit fat and sweaty.'

Sophie hung about for a few more minutes, looking increasingly distracted. Then she glanced at her watch. 'I have to tear myself away from your charming company,' she announced, looking pointedly at Anton.

His eyes followed her out of the room. When the door slammed, he said, 'She's a bit stuck-up, isn't she?'

Alex laughed. 'She likes you too, Anton.'

But Alex was pleased she had gone. Asking her along was a mistake. The others obviously felt awkward having her around listening to their stumbling efforts.

Unterleutnant Kohl was finishing a report on two students at the Humboldt-Universität who had been taking an unhealthy interest in the East Berlin uprising of 1953, when Colonel Theissen appeared at his door. 'Come and have a drink at the end of the day,' he instructed.

Kohl spent a restless few hours wondering if there was an ominous explanation for this meeting. Theissen was one of the few people in the world who frightened him. He had survived six years as a political prisoner in the infamous Nazi concentration camp at Dachau. When you spoke to him, his eyes bore right into you. They said he could sniff out secrets like a bloodhound. Kohl didn't like the idea of drinking with his boss. He thought it was a ploy to loosen his tongue. Theissen was usually so stiff and formal with his staff.

Kohl knocked on Theissen's door at the end of his shift. The Colonel was already relaxing and beckoned him to the padded easy chairs around a low table. He took a long drag on his cigarette and poured himself another whisky – a particularly nice bottle that had been confiscated from a consignment of foodstuffs and spirits some West Berliners had sent over to a relative in the East. He poured Kohl a generous measure.

'This is a challenging time for the Republik,' he told Kohl carefully. 'The Prague uprising has been a concern for the Politburo for the last four years. Comrade Minister Mielke tells me it has shaken them up more than they like to show. And the steps they're taking to ensure it does not happen in East Germany are far-reaching. We must be particularly mindful of Western influences – especially in the cultural sphere. Western rock music is corrupting our youth as surely as the CIA and the Voice of America.'

Kohl nodded. 'Today's youth walk a thin line – they flaunt their decadence. Even the children of the Party high-ups – they like to dress in the Western fashion. It's not right. They should be setting an example.'

Theissen nodded in agreement.

'The ones who are really out of line are easy enough to spot,' he said. 'And here, you are doing a valuable duty for your country – as important as your former placement in the International Section.'

He took out a press cutting recently confiscated on a record shop raid. 'Have you seen this lot?' He passed Kohl a photograph of Led Zeppelin. 'What was it Stalin said about the duty of the artist? To be "engineers of the human soul". I certainly wouldn't want these perverts corrupting the souls of our young people.'

'I feel unclean just looking at them,' said Kohl. 'Their parents must be the laughing stock of their district.'

CHAPTER 13

Sophie and Alex sat on a bench by Museum Island in the centre of Berlin, eating *Bockwurst* rolls. Alex's transistor radio – tuned to the West German pop station WDR1 – was playing quietly in his pocket. Sophie carried one too, and when a song they liked came on, they would plug their little earpieces in so they could listen in secret, turn up the volume, and tap along to the rhythm on each other's hands.

They were enjoying their Saturday. After the usual morning session at school, they had taken Grandma Ostermann shopping. It was a task Frank and Gretchen were increasingly reluctant to do. Grandma always complained about the quality of goods in East Berlin. In the grocer's that lunchtime she had announced that the food was better under the Nazis, even after the war started. And you didn't have to queue for it – at least not until the end.

The other shoppers tutted and Alex and Sophie had had to pretend they were shocked. 'That told them,' grinned Alex as they walked back to her apartment carrying her shopping.

'Did you see the look on their faces?' laughed Sophie.

Grandma looked smug – like a naughty school girl with a secret. As they left she slipped them a couple of Marks to thank them for their help and pinched them both on the cheek.

They were still laughing now, until Sophie decided it was time to break some bad news.

'Mutter and Vater have told me I am to stop seeing you. It's been very frosty at home recently – not that it was ever that different.' She gave a mirthless laugh. 'Mealtimes are the worst. Making conversation, it's like wading through treacle.' Her tone was matter of fact.

Alex looked at her with alarm, wondering what she was going to say next.

'Don't worry. I've been quite the delinquent about it. We've had some terrible rows. I've told them I'll leave home. Go and live with Auntie Rosemarie. Stop going to the Free German Youth meetings. So they relented. But they still want me to see less of you. Concentrate more on my schoolwork and cello lessons.'

Alex wasn't surprised. They froze him out on the rare occasions he visited her apartment now. He had started to call them 'The Grims'. Sophie understood. Fortunately, Alex's parents didn't mind her coming round to their home. They liked her. And Frank thought she was a good person for Alex to know – what with her parents' high standing in the Party.

'So, to keep the peace, perhaps I should not come to your rehearsals,' she said. 'If they're going to ration us, I'd rather see you on your own.' She reached for his hand. 'And maybe a *bit* less often?'

Alex nodded. He was relieved. He thought she had been going to dump him.

A couple of tiny sparrows arrived to pick up the crumbs from their lunch. Alex dropped a morsel of bread and one of them hopped beneath his feet to pick it up.

'Wouldn't it be great just to take to the sky and fly away,' said Sophie. 'They can have their breakfast in the West, lunch in the East and supper again in the West. Imagine that.'

It seemed such a simple, reasonable thing to do. But Alex could no more hope for that than he could wish to be Sandman and take his dinner on the Moon. He was stuck here on Planet Stasi, overseen by the evil eye of the TV Tower.

As they wandered through the streets on their way home they heard the rumble of the U-Bahn and felt a rustle of wind through a ventilation shaft, as a train from the West Berlin network rattled by beneath their feet. Stations on the lines that crossed from West to East were called *Geisterbahnhöfe* – 'ghost stations'. They were blocked off and manned by gun-toting guards.

'It's funny, isn't it,' said Sophie as the train rumbled by. 'Just a few metres down below there are people who are free to travel where they like and think and say whatever they want.'

As they walked home, Sophie told Alex about her new

job at the House of Ministries. The place had a sort of notoriety. It was in one of the Nazis' most famous buildings – the head office of Herman Goering's *Luftwaffe*. It had survived the war almost intact. These days it was a government administration centre. Sophie's Auntie Rosemarie worked there as a cleaner.

Alex was intrigued by her. Sophie had told him she was a bright woman but she had fallen foul of the regime in some way. It was considered impolite to even raise the subject. Sophie's aunt didn't like her job, but it paid the rent and kept her in bread rolls and schnapps. She had managed to get Sophie work there from time to time, when she wanted to make some extra money. Now they were asking Sophie if she wanted more regular work – Saturday afternoons mostly, but some evenings as well, if one of the women was ill.

'I hate being there in the evening, when everyone else has gone home,' she told Alex. 'Down in the basement, where the soldiers' barracks used to be, you can almost smell the sweat and the boot polish. When it's quiet, I sometimes think I can hear shouts from the parade ground and marching feet. It's haunted, that place. I'm sure of it.'

She paused. Alex knew she was dying to tell him something. 'What?' he said, elbowing her in the ribs.

'When you climb to the upper floors, you can see right over the Wall.'

Most of the buildings next to the eastern side of the Wall had been knocked down, but not the House of Ministries.

'So what does it look like?' he asked. Like most East

101

Berliners he was fascinated to know what lay behind the blank concrete face of the Eastern Wall. They didn't know anyone who had an apartment where you could see over it. He wondered if what he'd heard was true.

'There's one window with a perfect view,' said Sophie. 'Behind the Wall there's a great wide strip with trenches – to catch vehicles I suppose, and there are runs for the dogs. And there are tripwires which you can only see if the sun is shining in the right direction, and watchtowers and a lot of barbed wire. And on the other side there are buildings right next to the Wall.

'The other side's close enough to see people wave if they catch you staring out of the window. We're told very sternly not to wave back. The other night I spotted a little boy trundling along a side street on a tricycle, without a care in the world. I thought how nice it would be to be there on that side.'

They walked along for a few paces then Sophie's face lit up. 'I wonder how easy it would be to escape from that block?' she said excitedly. 'There probably isn't a better building in Berlin. I've been thinking about it as I dust and polish. You and me, we could hide in a lavatory after work, go up to the roof in the dead of night and get a rope over to the other side and slide down.'

Alex could not take her seriously. But he was thrilled she had put into words what he had not dared to tell her up on the Ferris wheel the other night. He looked at her and smiled. She didn't really mean it.

'I really mean it,' she said, suddenly serious. Alex felt a flash of fear. All at once he had a vivid image of himself, dangling like a fish on a line, being shot full of bullets as he tried to slide to freedom.

His face gave him away.

'Maybe it's too dangerous,' she said.

Alex held her tight. 'Maybe,' he said. 'Let's think about it.'

'There might be other ways to get away,' she said hurriedly. 'Maybe on the border rather than through Berlin? I heard the border security isn't as tight as it is in the city. Then there's a submarine that takes people through the Baltic . . .'

Alex squeezed her hand. 'You have been watching too much Western television,' he said, mimicking her father. 'Anyway, why do you want to escape? You've got a bright future here, haven't you? And you don't have to do military service!'

Her face fell and he wondered if he'd offended her. 'A bright, sparkling future, producing many children for the great Republik,' she said flatly. 'All of them exemplary socialist youth in their character and attitude and all of them destined for an identical green and brown apartment. I can barely wait. Do you want to spend the rest of your life living in a country whose politicians think putting different buttons on your jacket is "Western egotism"?'

* * *

Frank and Gretchen were wondering what Alex was up to. He had gone off with Sophie after school to visit Grandma Ostermann. He had been gone for hours now. They hoped he was not attracting the attention of the authorities.

They began to discuss their summer holidays. It was the perfect thing to do on a drab and cold spring day. They had their hopes pinned on the *Völkerfreundschaft* vacation ship. Every year, a thousand hand-picked citizens would take the luxury liner to Cuba for a fortnight in the sun. Only the most loyal and hard-working party members were selected. Frank and Gretchen always applied – they were no more or less deserving than any of the lucky few who went.

Failing that, they could go to the Baltic. Spend a week on Rügen Island and hope the weather was nice. Frank and Gretchen were both keen naturists. On holiday, as soon as the sun came out, they went straight to the beach and stripped off. Everyone did. There were few who dared to keep their swimming costumes on. For them it was a political gesture. Frank told his kids, 'We are all equal in society and never more so than when we are all naked on the beach.'

Alex and Geli didn't give it a second thought when they were younger, but they minded now. Especially when there were other teenagers about. Frank had taken to telling them they'd grow out of it.

At suppertime, when Alex had returned home, Frank raised the question of the summer holiday around the table. Alex and Geli looked shifty. They dreaded the day the letter would arrive telling them they had been chosen to go on a cruise. It would be great to get to travel abroad and they liked the idea of going to Cuba, but the thought of spending two weeks in close proximity to a bunch of Party robots whose conversation would revolve around the achievements of their plastering brigade on some building site was not appealing.

Alex had other things on his mind. Last year he had spent the school holiday working in an old people's home. He had mixed feelings about the work. He'd enjoyed talking to the residents but the prospect of spending the summer emptying chamber pots and trying to convince a confused old man that it was time to have a bath filled him with gloom. In the entrance hall there had been a gold-framed painting of Lenin – immaculate in suit and tie, surrounded by a sacred halo of light. It was the only thing about the place that was immaculate. The faded wallpaper behind the portrait, blotchy with damp, looked like it would peel off in one strip if you pulled on it.

'Vati, I have to get a job this summer holiday,' he said. 'What do you suggest?'

Frank thought for a minute. 'You need to talk to Herr Kalb. He's the head of the district building programme and a very good man to get to know. We have been Party comrades for years. He will be pleased to help you, I'm sure.'

Kalb was a staunch Party member. Alex didn't like him but Frank had a lot of time for Herr Kalb.

Student jobs had to be proper jobs – something messy

where you got yourself dirty like real workers and peasants. Nothing namby-pamby, like working in a library. The Party insisted on it. Even for those heading for university – they might be the brightest and the best but there was nothing like a down to earth summer job in a factory, farm, or construction site to remind a student that he or she was just like every one else.

Kalb had already told Frank Ostermann he would consider his son for a job. But Frank wanted Alex to ask himself. Show willing. Maybe he would join one of the high-rise construction projects. Kalb had told Frank you could put a whole eleven storey block up in 110 days, from muddy field to moving in. One flat every two or three days. Four families to a floor, it was a great step forward in the State's housing programme.

'The new housing,' Frank told Alex, 'is a perfect expression of our socialist life. All the same, no distinctions. All of us in this together.' Alex smiled at that. They certainly didn't live in the new housing and neither would they want to.

Alex decided he could put off the visit to Kalb no longer. He wondered whether if he got on well at the building site they would let him work in construction rather than join the army. He had heard a few kids were allowed to become 'construction soldiers' instead of having to go into the military. That was two years away but it still hung over him like a great black cloud.

They had been hearing about their army service in

school just the other day. This time Alex was listening. Herr Würfel told the class about the Wall. 'In a year or two, you boys will be called up for service in the National People's Army. There is every chance you will be one of those chosen to man the border towers. The guards who protect us consider it their patriotic duty to shoot any traitor who tries to breach the Protective Barrier.'

Alex had heard stories about how guards who didn't shoot were sent to the prison at Bautzen. And how those that did shoot were rewarded with extra leave and luxury goods – or better apartments for their families. How much was true he couldn't say, but he knew he couldn't shoot someone who was doing exactly what he would like to do himself.

Alex had a cousin who had recently finished his army service. 'If you are lucky, you'll spend eighteen months in a barracks in Dessau peeling potatoes and lighting farts for entertainment. That's what we had to do.'

'Sounds unmissable,' Alex had said, with a sinking feeling. 'At least we don't have a war to fight.'

He'd heard that the regular soldiers made a point of victimising the new recruits – sticking their heads down lavatory pans and stripping them naked and tying them to lamp posts in the middle of winter. Alex knew he'd have to toughen up a bit if he was going to survive conscription. Just thinking about it made him want to escape. If he played his cards right, Kalb could be his ticket away from all that.

* * *

Erich Kohl flexed his fingers and began tapping away at his typewriter.

```
Subject shows increasingly negative
attitude. Recent criminal activity
includes doggerel song lyric exhibiting
brazen false consciousness for unofficial
music ensemble 'Black Dog'. This attempt
to spread anti-State propaganda through
Western pop music plainest evidence yet
of negative-decadent tendencies and clear
betrayal of DDR.

"We're up against the Wall
and heading for a fall
But I'm still standing tall
Up against the Wall."

Ensemble's name 'Black Dog' — British
folklore term for deep depression —
clearly a reference to subject's own
internal psychosis regarding attitude to
living in DDR.

Suggest interventionist action.
```

CHAPTER 14

As Frank Ostermann approached his workplace, he was astonished to be confronted by three men who got out of an anonymous white car and asked him to accompany them. The older one, with the lank dark hair, had flashed an identity card at him, but too quickly for Frank to read it.

The car pulled into Stasi HQ at Normannenstrasse. Frank had seen the sprawling offices from the outside – a whole block's worth of buildings – but he had never imagined he would find himself on the other side of those road blocks and barbed wire.

They took him to a small white-walled room and gave him an uncomfortable chair to sit in. It seemed intentionally low off the ground – as if eight or nine centimetres had been sawn off the legs.

'I am at a complete loss as to why you have brought me here,' said Frank Ostermann. 'This is no way to treat a loyal Party member.'

Kohl didn't like his certainty. He'd soon put a stop to that. He showed him pictures of Alex and Geli. One was of Alex emerging from Holger Vogel's apartment block, the other of Geli out in the street.

'Why have you taken these photographs of my children?' said Frank. His voice betrayed his anxiety.

'You might be a loyal Party member, Herr Ostermann, but neither of your children have been a credit to you or your wife, Gretchen. Some might say that is ill fortune. Others might think this reflects badly on you as parents. I'm inclined to think it's the former, but my opinion is not what matters here.'

'What do you mean?' said Frank. He could feel his legs swimming in sweat as he sat in the plastic chair.

'Both Angela and Alexander have been under observation for some time,' said Kohl quietly. 'Neither has the correct socialist personality, and although there is currently no evidence of treasonable behaviour, there is strong suspicion. Enough to warrant arrest and incarceration. You have a duty to the State to ensure they become useful comrades. If you wish to discuss their behaviour with me, you may contact me here. My name is Erich Kohl.'

As soon as Frank left the room his chair was wiped down with a thick cotton cloth, which was placed in a glass jar, sealed, labelled and filed away.

Kohl escorted him to the exit out on Normannenstrasse and left him standing on the pavement. 'You can make your own way back,' said Kohl as he released his hold on Frank's arm. 'And not a word to anyone. Even your family. We will know if you tell them.'

Frank stood watching the sparse traffic shoot past and wondered whether or not he should say anything to his family about what had happened. He had tried to warn Alex and Geli. What else could he do? Make them stop watching West German television? He could hardly pin Alex down and cut his hair. He felt an overwhelming sense of shame and had to bite his lip to hold back the tears that welled up inside him.

CHAPTER 15

Alex took the morning off school to meet Herr Kalb at the district housing office. It was a cold damp day and his tram smelled of wet dog. He looked down the crowded carriage at all the dowdy overcoats and fur hats, faces staring straight ahead or at the grey condensation on the windows. Was he going to look like this in twenty or thirty years' time? They said that there would be communism in space by then and no further need for money. But nothing would have changed though, Alex thought. Everyone would still be riding dirty buses wearing the same disgruntled expressions.

He wiped the condensation away and peered out of the window. The street was as tatty as most of the others in this area of East Berlin. Half cobble stone and half tarmac – hasty repairs after the war when the original cobbles had been blown to pieces by Soviet artillery. The older buildings – the ones that had survived the bombing and the fighting – were still peppered with bullet marks.

Alex noticed one which was particularly badly scarred by bullets and wondered who had died in there. Maybe it had been some *Hitler-Jugend* boys his own age. His grandma had spoken of how they had fought against the Russians.

Alex could imagine how terrifying it must have been to be trapped inside that house and then have the windows smashed to pieces by a hail of machine-gun fire. All the bullets and splinters of glass flying about. Then a grenade or the scorching tongue of a flame-thrower. He flinched at the thought. What a way to die.

Alex reached his stop and got off. As the tram rolled away he saw a familiar face at the window caught in a sudden shaft of bright spring sunshine. He could swear it was that man. The one he had seen in the park. He was sure he'd been following him. The fellow stared straight at him – the way adults did with naughty children.

The district housing office was a short walk from the tram stop. Kalb saw Alex at once. He had a head of thick black hair, with a great quiff at the front, held in place with some slightly whiffy oil, pompadour style. He was wearing a white nylon shirt and black tie, and he stank of body odour. They talked about football, and the chances of *Dynamo Berlin* being knocked from the top of the *DDR-Oberliga*. Alex got the impression that Herr Kalb wasn't terribly busy.

The meeting was a success. Kalb said he was sure Alex would be as reliable as his father and he would be pleased to offer him work in the summer break. It wouldn't be very exciting. Mixing concrete. Carrying buckets of plaster. Heaving round prefabricated slabs. That sort of thing.

Alex left the office feeling light-hearted. It would be great to have a job like that over the long vacation. It would be good to be out in the sunshine. And Herr Kalb seemed like a nice man. Alex felt guilty about not liking him before.

When Alex arrived at school, he was called over by the receptionist. She sat behind an elaborate art deco iron grille inside an elegant curved portal. In contrast, the interior of her office had flaking grey paint, with a portrait of Honecker on the wall behind her.

The woman herself was as dour as her office walls, with thinning black hair tied in a tight bun. She wore a nylon floral apron. 'You must report at once to the Principal,' she commanded.

Alex went to Herr Roth's office and knocked timidly on the door. Roth told him to sit down and then went into his secretary's office to rummage around in a filing cabinet.

Alex stared at the contents of Roth's desk and wondered what was coming next. Roth had a pen set featuring a small globe resting on a red star stand with the flags of the Eastern Bloc countries arranged around the curved support. A thrusting golden fist emerged from the North Pole. That was communism all right, thought Alex. A fist punching its way right through the world, screwing everything up.

Roth returned. Without prevarication he announced that Alex's applications for the *Erweiterte Oberschule* and teacher training at vocational school had both been rejected. There was no way he would be able to train as a teacher now. 'When the machinery is not running smoothly, we have to replace the parts that don't work,' he said.

'You know I'm one of the brightest students in my year,'

Alex said plainly. There was no point in being modest, it was true. Herr Roth looked appalled at this.

'And you know how well I have been doing, teaching the kids down in Schöneweide. My work experience reports have always been excellent.'

Roth was unmoved. 'You have plainly failed to show political-moral maturity, or any sense of unity with the DDR. Your false opinions and uncertainty can only be seen as moral transgressions against our country. And for that reason I cannot recommend your entry to further education. You may perform well in your work experience school under supervision but you cannot be trusted on your own with the moral and political well-being of our children.'

'So what am I supposed to do?' said Alex. He was beginning to realise the enormity of his problem. Being the son of loyal and well-connected Party members wasn't going to help him after all.

'You can go back to the careers office and ask them to find you some information on the less skilled aspects of the chemical industry. There'll always be work for people in our country, Alex, even for someone like you.'

That was Alex's cue to leave.

That day he walked out of the school with a horrible sinking feeling. The chemistry teacher, Herr Unger, had recently been telling them about the benefits of the East German chemistry industry.

'Chemistry produced bread, prosperity and beauty,' said Herr Unger just as he threw his chalk at Alex, who had not been paying attention. 'All the things you, Master Ostermann, will find missing from your life if you carry on failing to apply yourself to your education.'

As he went to unlock his bike Alex noticed the rear tyre was flat again. He got as far as taking the inner tube out and trying to find the puncture when he realised the valve had been tampered with. The tyre had been deliberately deflated. By the time he'd finished putting it back on the wheel and pumping it up, his shirt was stained with mud and oil and he had broken a fingernail. He cursed the whole way home.

Alex decided he was not going to tell his mother and father about the school's decision to bar him from further education. He would go back to talk to Herr Roth. Try to get him to change his mind. They were just frightening him. Trying to get him to toe the line. And it had worked. He must change.

When Alex explained why it had taken him so long to get back from school, Geli looked perplexed. 'Someone did that to my bike too,' she said.

'Well, aren't you both the lucky ones!' said Gretchen with a laugh. 'Who have you been annoying recently?' Alex and Geli looked at each other but they didn't say anything until they were alone.

'Maybe it's just a coincidence?' whispered Geli. She wasn't convinced. Alex could hear it in her voice. 'If it was just you, I'd think Nadel or that boy who was after

Sophie was having a go at you, but the both of us . . . that's bizarre.'

'Maybe one of your old boyfriends is nursing a grudge?' said Alex.

She shrugged. 'I can't imagine who.'

Then Alex told her what was really on his mind.

'I think they've really got it in for me,' he said. 'I've been barred from vocational school or the *Erweiterte Oberschule.*'

Geli looked appalled. 'WHAT?' she shouted, and Alex had to hush her.

'How am I going to tell Vati and Mutti?'

'They'll find out,' said Geli. 'Better tell them. Otherwise they'll be twice as angry with you. Anyway, Vati might be able to have a word with the right people.' Then she put her hand on his shoulder. 'Alex, what are you going to do? You can't spend your life working in the refuse department at the chemical works or sweeping the streets. It'll drive you mad.'

Alex said he would talk to Herr Roth in a few days. Try to get him to change his mind. Then if that failed he would ask his father to have a quiet word. 'Maybe I should join the Free German Youth again?' he said with a horrible sinking feeling.

Geli snorted. 'They might not have you!' Then she said, 'You know, I've got problems too. Fuhrmann – that new art teacher – is telling me my work isn't up to scratch and I'm never going to be good enough to go to college. Herr Lang used to tell me I was the best in the school.'

Alex shook his head. 'What shall we do?'

Geli shrugged. 'Keep our heads down? I don't know . . .'

Over the next week there were terrible rows in the house with Frank. He had decided, completely out of the blue, to forbid them all to watch Western television. He talked about 'the corrupting influence of the capitalist lifestyle' and 'the false consciousness of our class enemy' and even Gretchen told him he was beginning to sound like one of Honecker's speeches.

'But the Party says we're allowed to,' Geli and Alex both said.

Frank found it difficult to argue with them both at once. 'I don't care,' he shouted. 'It is still unpatriotic and it is bad for your reputation if you ever come to your senses and decide you want to join the Party.'

Stranger things were happening away from their apartment. Geli and Alex both found their bikes had been tampered with yet again – usually the tyres, but sometimes the seat or handlebars had been loosened. It was quite dangerous. But both of them decided they would carry on going out on their bikes. It was a matter of principle. Someone had it in for them and they were determined to show them they were not going to be intimidated. Now neither of them went out on their bike without a toolkit.

But one day in early June, when Alex took his bike to a nearby café and left it in view as he sat in the window with Sophie, he saw the culprit. After ten minutes a large, solid man of middle years came along and began to fiddle with the tyres. He made no pretence of seeing if anyone was watching him. He just crouched down and did it without even looking around.

Alex thought to go out and challenge him, but Sophie grabbed his hand. 'Don't be silly,' she said. 'He's obviously Stasi. And he looks pretty tough too. He'll just beat you up. Don't do it, Alex.'

Alex couldn't believe what he was seeing. 'Here we are, caught between the Yanks and the Ivans, we're all a whisker away from being blown to pieces, and what does our glorious Republik spend its time doing? Harassing sixteen-year-old boys with long hair. What a crap country.'

People were staring now. Sophie hushed him.

The bike stuff was ridiculous, but Alex didn't really care about it. What did upset him, and Geli too, was that most of their friends stopped talking to them. Kids in the school yard that Alex would hang out with at breaktime began to freeze him out when he went to sit with them. Heinz announced he was no longer available to play with the band. Anton still got together with him to play but even with him there was something missing. That easy camaraderie they had seemed to have evaporated.

'Have they been on to you too?' Alex asked Sophie, when they were talking about the behaviour of his former friends. 'Asked you to spy on me?'

She looked him in the eye. 'Don't you think I would have told you?' she chided.

119

'We've got to get out of this place,' he said.

Sophie smiled and sang the next line of the pop song they both knew from the West German radio.

He walked Sophie back to her apartment, which was in an old ivy-clad block.

'Climb up in the night. I'll leave a window open,' she said, trying to cheer him up.

Alex loved the idea of secretly spending the night with Sophie, though he wasn't sure he was up to scaling five storeys without falling off and breaking his neck.

He returned home to find his father in a black mood. Frank had drunk most of a bottle of schnapps and could barely move from his chair. Perhaps he had had a bad day at work. Alex went to bed early but could not sleep for thinking about what Sophie had said about escaping. Maybe he would go to the Ministries building and take a look. It made him feel sick with nerves just thinking about trying to escape. He definitely didn't want them to be the next Holger and Effi.

What happened next was more sinister. On her Christmas visit last year, Gretchen's Aunt Magdalene, who had married a Frenchman and lived in Lyon, surprised them by bringing the children each a set of cotton underwear. Seven pairs of underpants and knickers. She apologised for giving them such a dull gift but they were both delighted.

Geli had been the first to notice. 'Someone's stolen a

pair of my knickers,' she said. Alex laughed when she told him. A couple of summers back they'd had a strange young man coming round the block stealing underwear from washing lines. He'd been arrested and sent to prison.

'I keep track of those knickers,' she said. 'Best ones I've got.' Then she said, 'One of your pervy friends hasn't stolen them, has he?'

Alex was indignant. Anton had been round recently but he couldn't imagine him doing anything like that.

Alex went back to his room. He looked under his bed in the place where he kept the Led Zeppelin record that Sophie had lent him. It was gone. He went straight back to Geli's room. They had an irate whispered conversation where he accused her of taking it without asking him. Geli was livid with him for making such an accusation, but Alex returned to his room convinced she had lent it to her boyfriend, Jan-Carl, without asking him.

Then on laundry day Alex counted out his pants and there were six rather than seven. He felt a shiver of revulsion.

'They've been in here, haven't they?' he said to Geli. 'They've broken in to our apartment and stolen our underwear. It's the sort of thing you expect some pervert to do, not your own government.'

They both felt sick about it. They'd heard rumours that the Stasi had a great collection of clothing belonging to people who were politically suspect. They kept the clothes in sealed jars in what was known as a 'smell pantry'. If they were hunting a known subversive who had gone on the run, they would retrieve a jar from the smell pantry and wave its contents under the noses of the tracker dogs.

They wondered whether or not to tell their parents. Alex cautioned Geli not to. His father had been drinking solidly for the last few weeks. Every night he stumbled to bed in a fug of alcohol fumes. If he thought the Stasi had been breaking into their apartment because of Alex, he would be absolutely furious.

Erich Kohl was sifting through a cardboard box containing a small selection of items removed from the Ostermann's apartment. He picked up the record sleeve with the picture of an old man carrying a bundle of sticks on the front.

'Look at this,' he told a colleague who was helping him catalogue the haul. 'It belongs to the boy. I recognised it at once. Led Zeppelin. Remember that name. Devious nonsense from a bunch of shrieking monkeys. The name of the group is not even printed on the record sleeve. That has to be deliberate subterfuge.' He took the vinyl record from the sleeve. 'But look, they have printed it on the record itself. They're not as clever as they think.'

He placed the record and its sleeve in a plastic evidence bag.

'He's sailing very close to the wind, this one,' Kohl confided. 'One more transgression and we'll be bringing him in.'

CHAPTER 16

'Come to the Ministries building with me,' asked Sophie again. 'I get bored. It'd be nice to have a bit of company. We can say you're helping out, to cover one of the girls who's sick.'

'Won't it be difficult to get in?' said Alex. The idea excited and scared him in equal measure.

Sophie shook her head. 'The guards on the door are a pretty thick lot.'

Alex thought it would be fun to go along. He could spend a bit more time with Sophie and it sounded like an adventure. So the next time she did a weekday evening at the House of Ministries he came along with her.

'Ingeborg's got the flu,' Sophie said to the guard. 'He's come to help us out.' He seemed to find that an acceptable reason to let Alex in without a pass.

'Who's Ingeborg?' asked Alex as Sophie unlocked the storage cupboard where they kept the cleaning equipment.

'She usually does the weekends,' she whispered and tossed him over a broom. 'Make yourself look useful with a bit of sweeping up.'

Alex swept the floors. Was this what the rest of his life

was going to be like? He wondered again if it was too late to start toeing the line and behave like a good socialist youth. He had kept putting off his visit to plead with Herr Roth. His mum and dad were right. There were rules. You didn't have to believe in them, but you had to stick to them. Do and say what they wanted you to do and say, but still carry on being yourself in your own apartment. He decided he would definitely go to talk to Roth on Monday. Try to set things right.

He looked over to see Sophie leaning forward to dust a window. Even in a pink overall she looked lovely.

After an hour they stopped to share a coffee she had brought in a flask.

'Want to have a look at that window?' she asked. 'The one where you can see over the Wall.'

Alex grinned. It seemed like a wonderfully mischievous thing to do. He didn't really think he and Sophie would be able to escape. He was only here for a laugh.

Ten minutes later she came up to him. 'Coast is clear. Let's have a look . . .'

They made their way as quickly and quietly as they could up a couple of flights of marble stairs. Sophie went ahead, pointed at a window on the corridor and said, 'Ta-dah!'

Alex stared open-mouthed at the Western side. He could see cars – all different colours rather than just black or pastel blue or green. Some were even two colours at once. Imagine that! Also there on the other side was the

Europahaus building – a 1930 high-rise that looked almost contemporary. Alex remembered seeing it in a textbook. It was a beautiful sight – elegant and distinctive and with no sign of the ugly war damage that still blighted many buildings in the East.

His attention was drawn back to the Wall, which was right under the window. He could see trenches and dog runs and barbed wire and lighting gantries and minefields and watchtowers – just as Sophie had said. He understood at once how fatal it would be to try to cross it. Like most East Berliners, Alex had never seen what lay behind the blank face of the Wall.

'We could do it,' said Sophie, as she placed her chin on his shoulder. They stared out of the window together. 'We could get a rope and throw it over and slide down. We could!'

Alex wanted to mock her but he hated to dent her enthusiasm.

'Here, comrade. Got any rope?' he said, trying to let her down gently. 'How are we going to find a rope long enough to do that?'

'There are ladders – rope ladders – in a storeroom at the top of the building. I found them when I was cleaning up there. For if there's a fire, I suppose.'

In both directions the Wall stretched as far as the eye could see. It was there: like the sky and the trees and night and day. What was so strange was seeing buildings with people in them on the other side. They were close enough to shout over to. But they were a completely different species: *Homo go-where-the-hell-you-want-iens*. Provided they had enough money, they could spin a globe, point to anywhere on it and take off. His countrymen couldn't even go to the rest of their own capital city without a stamp of approval from the Stasi.

Alex imagined him and Sophie, there on the other side, making plans to travel to London or Los Angeles or New York or anywhere they wanted. Somewhere where you wouldn't get called a class traitor and locked up for wanting to travel. They were so close, there by the window, he could almost taste what it was like to be free.

His train of thought was interrupted by the sound of boots running on a marble floor. Alex looked up to see two security guards hurtling towards him, guns in their hands. He stood up and wondered why they felt the need to draw their guns. Both of the men were heavily overweight and they could barely speak by the time they got to him.

'Against the wall,' gasped one of them as they frisked him down.

'What's the problem?' said Sophie, who had decided boldness was the best approach. 'He's helping me out.'

'You're out of a job here, Fräulein,' said one of the men sharply. 'You're both coming down to the police station.'

Ten minutes later they had been locked in separate cells and Alex cursed himself for not thinking up a cover story. He thought of his father's words: *You in your invincible youth! You think nothing can touch you and nothing can go wrong.*

Alex was beginning to realise that Frank was right some of the time.

They kept him in there for an hour before manhandling him into a small concrete room with a desk and two chairs. The desk held a tape recorder and desk lamp. Behind it sat a lean, unsmiling, middle-aged man who looked at him with open hostility.

The interrogation was more brutal than Alex had expected. The cops had been relatively civil with them when they brought them in. But now he was being questioned by this hard-faced brute who told him that Sophie had confessed he had bullied her into getting him into the building. Threatened to beat her if she did not let him.

'What sort of *Arschloch* threatens to beat his own girlfriend?' said the man.

Alex didn't believe that, but it did make him wonder what she had really said.

'Why were you at the House of Ministries, Alex Ostermann?'

'I was helping my girlfriend out with her cleaning job. Her parents don't like me and we're never allowed to spend any time together.'

The man looked at his file. 'Don't . . . like . . . you,' he said slowly. 'I'm not surprised.' He stood up holding a page from the file and read from it as he walked behind Alex. '"Asocial", "lacking political-moral maturity", "holding false opinions", "corrupting upstanding socialist youth", "making malicious propaganda against the State" . . .' He yanked Alex's hair hard. Alex let out a yell, more out of surprise than fear. 'I don't like you either.'

The man continued to walk around Alex, uncomfortably close to him. Then he stood right behind him. Alex grew increasingly tense. He thought the man was going to hit him.

Instead he put his face close to Alex's ear.

'We think you're a spy, Alex Ostermann,' he said quietly, then returned to the other side of the desk. 'Gathering intelligence at government offices.'

'Do you know what happens to spies?' he said as he sat down and made his hand into the shape of a gun. He put it to his temple and said, '*PK-KOW*', jolting his head to mimic the impact of the bullet. Alex wondered if he had actually shot someone like that.

'We're going to keep you here for a while,' he said. 'See what else your girlfriend tells us.'

Alex was returned to solitary confinement. He was feeling deeply confused. Did they believe his story? Why did they think he was a spy? Then there was the 'making malicious propaganda against the State'. What the hell was *that* all about? Did they mean his band? How would *they* know about *that*? No one had accused him of planning to escape. That was the most obvious thing, but they hadn't even mentioned it.

They didn't keep him there a while at all. After a night in his cell he was taken by car to Hohenschönhausen detention centre in the east of the city.

CHAPTER 17

The smell of the place hit him as soon as he arrived. A sharp high whiff of disinfectant and then a lower stale note – the sickly miasma of sweat and human waste. Alex knew that smell well enough from last summer, from the old people's nursing home. But all the residents in this particular wing of the prison were youths.

Then there was the noise. A sort of muffled clamour, like a crowded swimming pool. The clang of steel doors, the crack of boots on concrete floors, echoing around with the shouts and murmurs of the inmates.

The guards took him to a room with blank whitewashed walls and a tiny barred window set close to the ceiling. A concrete recess in the wall made do for a bed. No mattress. No chair. Nothing, apart from a bucket on the floor.

After half an hour – at least he assumed it was half an hour, it could have been ten minutes – he started to imagine people whispering to him, or the walls moving a little, throbbing in the harsh light of the fluorescent strip in the ceiling.

Alex fretted. His stomach shrank to a tight little knot. Eventually they came to get him. 'Break any of the prison rules and you go back in there for a week. Try to hit one of us and it's a month,' said the guard.

They issued him with a prison uniform with 254 stencilled on the back. It was slightly too big for him, felt scratchy and smelled of stale sweat. Then they marched him off without a word, before he could even turn back the sleeves.

The next stop was the prison barber and Alex began to struggle and shouted when he realised what was coming. So they threw him into a solitary cell. This one was worse than the one he had just been in. Rubber-padded, complete sound insulation, no chair, no bed, pitch black, with the all-pervasive tang of disinfectant. After an hour Alex thought he could hear someone or something breathing in the cell and he had to fight really hard to keep his panic at bay. 'Don't be stupid,' he told himself. 'This is just a cell. There was nothing else here when you came in and there's nothing come in since. Breathe deeply. Keep calm. Don't let them win. This is a prison. It's not a horror film.'

When his breathing returned to normal, he began to feel an extraordinary tiredness. The events of the last couple of days caught up with him. He lay down on the hard cold floor and drifted into dreamless sleep.

Alex was disconcerted to wake up and discover he was still there and there was no difference between having his eyes open and having them closed. A cold draught was coming from somewhere. At least the cell had some ventilation. That was good because there was an awful stench of rubber there.

Alex needed to pee. He remembered seeing the outline of a bucket in the corner before the door slammed and he reached for it on his hands and knees, carefully feeling his way in the darkness. When his fingers made contact with cold tin, he peed as carefully as he could and put the bucket in the far corner – somewhere where he was unlikely to knock it over.

Now he was beginning to feel uneasy. He had no idea how long they had kept him in there. An hour – all morning?

There was a rattle and the door swung open. The light blinded him and he instinctively cringed, expecting to be hit.

'Out,' barked a guard. There were two of them. Young men in their twenties. They looked on him with cold, hard faces, grabbed him either side and frogmarched him away.

'What's happening?' said Alex. 'Where am I going?'

'Prisoner 254, no talking,' said one, gripping Alex's arm so tightly he could feel it going numb.

Alex shut up. He was in quite enough trouble already.

They took him to the barber and left him on his own. The barber was big enough to take care of himself. Alex expected him to be just as curt, but he surprised him by being nice. Well, not nice exactly, but like a kindly parent who was explaining to a naughty child why they had been punished. Alex began to feel tearful.

'Prison rules,' explained the barber. '"No prisoner shall be permitted to wear hair longer than accepted military length,"' he rattled off, in the slightly mocking way people use to quote official regulations they don't really agree with.

'If you're an enemy of the State, we should try to change you,' he said and ruffled Alex's hair. 'You're here to be reformed, not just punished. So first we will try to make you look like a defender of the State. After all, in a couple of years' time you will be expected to join our armed forces and protect your country.'

Alex didn't know what to make of this. The man was gentle with him and had a slightly camp manner – like one of those TV presenters on variety programmes that all the old ladies loved. He noticed his own hair gathering in wispy clumps around his feet and fought back his tears.

'Chin up, lad,' said the barber. Then he leaned closer, pressed something into Alex's hand and whispered, 'Couple of sweets for later. Give one of them to someone you like the look of. It's useful to have a friend in here.'

Fortunately there were no mirrors in the prison so Alex did not have to worry about what he looked like. And when he was marched back to the ordinary cells no one looked at him twice. Actually, Alex admitted to himself, having his hair cut was a blessing. Now the other prisoners would not know at once that he had just arrived.

Except they would. The ones who had been here for a

while had a pale, pasty look about them – like white bread left out in the sun that was starting to curl at the edges. Alex was too brown – too healthy-looking.

Before they got to his cell a bell went and the other boys hurried down to the canteen to eat.

'Go with them,' said the guard. 'We'll sort you out afterwards.'

Alex watched the others and copied them exactly. He grabbed a tray and picked up a spoon and lined up in the queue for the serving counter. There were no knives or forks here. It was too easy to imagine them being used as a weapon. Alex looked at his spoon and thought you could still do a good job poking someone's eye out with the handle.

He felt a jabbing in his back. He turned round to see a wiry, ratty-looking boy about his age and size. 'You look like a soft egg,' the boy said in a low voice. 'Ripe for a beating.'

There were two others with this boy, both grinning and snickering. Alex wondered what he was supposed to do. Did you ignore these taunts or did you react immediately? If he hit him, he'd be in serious trouble again.

'Shut up, Maier,' shouted a prison guard. 'If I catch you talking in the canteen queue again, you're off to solitary.'

'Yes, sir,' barked the ratty boy and stood to attention. It was difficult to know whether he was mocking the guard or genuinely frightened of him.

The wait in the queue was interminable. All the while they whispered 'soft egg' and 'creep' at Alex. He gritted his teeth and tried to ignore them. The food looked awful. Some sort of gristly pinkish mince with vegetables that had been boiled to a pulp. He spotted a single chair at the end of a table and went to sit down. The other boys there totally ignored him – which was preferable.

Despite the vileness of the food Alex was hungry and he ate quickly. After he'd drunk his third glass of water he began to worry about where he was going next. A bell went – so loud and piercing it made his ears hurt – and the boys all got up and placed their trays and plates in racks. Alex made sure he kept well away from the ones who had taunted him in the queue. Please, please, he implored a nebulous deity, don't put me in a cell with them.

They filed out back to the holding room and one of the guards caught Alex by the arm and dragged him out of the human stream. 'Wait here,' he said.

As he stood at the side, one of the ratty boy's friends could not resist a final insult. 'Creep,' he said as he passed, punching Alex on the arm, just as the guard returned.

The guard dragged the boy out. 'You are going to solitary,' Alex heard him say.

He felt sick. Now they would have even more reason to persecute him.

The prisoners marched to their cell doors and waited outside, leaving Alex to stand there alone. He was feeling very conspicuous and could sense them all looking at him.

A guard called them to attention and there was a head-count and roll-call.

When the guard called out 'Fiedler', another guard called 'Detention'.

That must be the boy's name. The one who had hit him. Alex was alarmed to hear a mutinous murmur from the other boys. He could not make out what it meant. Were they sorry for Fiedler or glad he would be out of the way for a while?

A guard came and took Alex down a long marble corridor with a highly polished floor. 'In here, 254,' said the guard and ushered him into a cell. Alex took a deep breath and entered.

CHAPTER 18

Alex's heart was thumping hard in his chest. He was trying his best to hide his fear. As the door swung open he peered in. There were two bunk beds, a chair and table, and a portable toilet. That was why the whole place smelled so bad. The cells all had their own portable toilets. So far he could not see anyone else in there.

'Hartmann, say *Guten Tag* to your cellmate,' said the guard.

A young man lying on the top bunk sat up, then jumped down.

'You must be Alex,' he said, as he shook his hand.

Alex couldn't believe his luck.

'I'm Eugen Hartmann.'

The guard slammed the door and locked it.

'That's it until supper,' said Eugen. 'It gets very boring. I'll give you a tour of the facilities. Here we have the bookshelf . . .'

He pointed to three dusty, moth-eaten old books. Alex scanned the titles: *Creating Young Comrades*; Nikolai Ostrovsky's *How the Steel Was Tempered*; and *Scientific Socialism, Victor of History*. There were also several ragged copies of the *Sputnik* youth magazine.

'Not an inspired choice, but they're the best I could find,' said Eugen. 'You'll read anything after you've been stuck here for a week.'

'How long have you been here?' asked Alex.

'Just over a week,' said Eugen.

Alex wondered if he should ask why Eugen was in here.

'They put me here for selling black market records,' said Eugen.

'Cool,' said Alex. He liked him already.

'I don't know how long I'm going to stay here. They've forbidden me to mix with the others. Say I'm a bad influence. They must think you're corrupt enough already for it not to matter!'

Alex was so relieved to meet someone who seemed OK. He reached into his pocket and offered him a sweet. Eugen smiled and popped it in his mouth.

'I don't really know why they put me in here. Being awkward, I think,' swaggered Alex. 'And listening to the wrong music.'

'They must have thought we'd have a lot to talk about,' said Eugen with a laugh.

They did too – long into the afternoon. Most of it was about their favourite rock groups and who played the best guitar. Eugen was a Hendrix fan and looked down his nose at Led Zeppelin. 'They stole all their best tunes from the old blues guys,' he said. ' "The Lemon Song" – that's "Killing Floor" by Howlin' Wolf. "Whole Lotta Love" – that's "You Need Love" by Willie Dixon.'

Alex didn't know enough about it to argue, but he had heard one or two of 'the old blues guys' and Led Zeppelin sounded nothing like them.

Eugen was good company – Alex had been lucky. The only thing he hated about being in that cell with Eugen was that there was a single portable toilet in the corner. He felt embarrassed when he needed to take a crap.

'It's just like kindergarten,' said Eugen, 'but with just one potty.'

Alex laughed as he remembered his kindergarten days. They used to make them all sit on their potties at the same time. It was something about encouraging them to be good citizens. No one was allowed off until all of them had finished.

'Still – at least we have a proper portable toilet,' said Eugen. 'Some cells just have a bucket.'

'Do you ever think about getting out of here?' said Eugen quietly.

'What, you mean digging a tunnel or throwing a grappling hook over the wall?' Alex laughed. 'Maybe we could smuggle ourselves out in the laundry basket!'

Eugen smiled. 'No, I meant getting out of the DDR. Don't you get sick of it?'

All at once Alex realised Eugen might not be quite who he thought he was. People who had only just met didn't talk to each other like this. So he considered his reply very carefully. 'I don't know. When I think of all the things I'd like to do . . . then yes I do. But when I think about the other stuff – my family and friends, how badly they treat you at work in the West, how they don't look after their old people, how expensive everything is, all that selfishness and backstabbing, I think it's better to be here.'

Eugen smiled. 'That's just what they want you to think. I'd go tomorrow if they let me.'

'All these rules and restrictions,' said Alex. 'That's what drives me mad. And this.' He gestured around the cell indignantly. 'I can't believe I'm an enemy of the State.'

He was talking louder the more exasperated he got. Eugen shushed him.

Alex wondered how long they were going to keep him in prison. He was called out for his evening meal and when he returned Eugen was no longer there. He had left a small note under Alex's pillow. 'Being transferred. Keep rockin', E.'

Alex kept expecting another cellmate to arrive but no one did and he spent the night on his own. He wondered who else had been in this cell and how close to despair and suicide they might have been. He remembered the little lecture he had received when he arrived. 'You will be deprived of your belt and shoelaces. But should you attempt to take your own life in any other way while you are in custody, this will be regarded as an attempt to avoid punishment and you will be treated accordingly.'

He was also weighed down with anxiety. Who would be joining him in here next? What would Geli and his mum and dad be thinking? And what were they doing to Sophie?

139

The report was sitting on Erich Kohl's desk when he
arrived at work early the next morning.

Alex Ostermann 254
Observation statement
Hohenschönhausen

Subject shows incorrect and delusional
aspirations and embryonic delinquency
with pronounced negative-decadent
tendencies, but is not a potential class
enemy or likely imperialist espionage
operative. Feelings towards DDR and
Federal Republic are fluid and malleable.

Recommend further preventative harassment
and continued day to day monitoring as
may still be vulnerable to hostile and
negative influences and oppositional
thinking but further contained
supervision is unnecessary. With correct
course of action subject can still be
regarded as potential comrade. May also
be possible in near future to inveigle
subject into own monitoring collaboration
as he is well placed to report on other
asocials within his circle. More
information needed on likely reliabilty/

unreliabilty as potential unofficial
collaborator.

Kohl added his own additional information to the file:

Sophie Kirsch

Accomplice to Ostermann in potential
adversarial asocial activity. Previous
exemplary record as model socialist youth
suggests subject might be suitable
assistant to preventative action. Suggest
coercive or persuasive approach,
depending on degree of false-
consciousness exhibited.

Report on reliability of Ostermann
parents and other family members

Parents have unimpeachable record as
supporters of DDR and SED. Both m and f
have been Party members since 1965. No
question of negative influence and
necessity of subject's removal to
politically reliable foster family.

Only possible negative influence is sister
Angela, aka Geli. Past record of

```
association with negative-decadents (now
terminated), but work in photography
course shows potential harmful tendencies
and reluctance to stay within boundaries
of socialist realism.
```

Kohl scribbled a note for the department secretary to telex back to Hohenschönhausen and shouted out for her to come into his office and fetch it. He watched her leave the room with her haughty nose in the air. She had responded with complete indifference to his earlier flirtations. So now Kohl amused himself with little acts of humiliation.

He regarded the report with some scepticism. Comrade Minister Mielke had told them they had a duty to the State to 'creep under the skin' of such potential class traitors and imperialist collaborators and 'look into their hearts so that we can reliably know who they are and where they stand'. Kohl knew exactly where Alex Ostermann stood. He was a straightforward negative-decadent – his fantasies revolved around playing a guitar in front of an adoring audience, not bringing down the enemies of the DDR. For a moment his impatience got the better of him.

Then he started to think more logically. He had a duty to the State to reclaim the socialist soul of Alex Ostermann. Maybe he was worrying too much about that cock-up with the Red Army Faction, but he couldn't afford to give them any reason to doubt his own commitment.

CHAPTER 19

Alex had the strangest dream. He followed Eugen down a road close to Treptower Park. Eugen did not know Alex was right behind him and had stopped at every bicycle he found and let down the tyres. Alex started to tell people in the street what he was doing but they all ignored him.

When he woke at dawn, Alex immediately went through everything he could remember about his conversations with Eugen. Had he said too much? Had he said anything they didn't know about him already? Eugen had asked several leading questions. Even then, Alex had started to feel a little uneasy about his cellmate. Now, looking back, everything was too convenient: Eugen saying he was not allowed to mix with the prison population, his 'transfer' after an afternoon in the cell.

Alex decided he had been wise to hold his tongue – especially about his desire to get out of the country. He tried to read *Scientific Socialism, Victor of History*, to keep his mind from spinning round and round.

He had only just got back to sleep, it seemed, when the wake-up bell sounded. Alex dressed and washed rapidly, to be ready for the summons for breakfast, and wondered anxiously what the day held in store. But before the breakfast bell rang there was a commotion at the door and three guards came in.

'Prisoner 254,' said one with sergeant stripes on his arm. 'You are to come with us.'

They handcuffed him tight behind his back and then two of the guards marched him down the corridor. They took him up two flights of stairs and then down two more and out through a courtyard into a section of the prison he had not seen before.

'What's happening?' he asked.

'No talking,' said the guards.

They arrived at a small building at the perimeter of the prison and stopped in front of the entrance. 'Hold still,' commanded one of the guards, and then knelt down in front of Alex and tied his ankles together with a small rope.

'What are you doing?' he asked anxiously.

'In we go,' said the guard and opened the door. Two others picked him up by his arms.

Inside the building was a single room with whitewashed walls and a plain stone floor. The building smelled of wood oil and disinfectant. In one corner there was a great black curtain. One of the guards drew back the curtain with a dramatic flourish. A guillotine stood before them.

Alex took one look at the nightmare machine and the blood drained from his face. 'You can't do this to me!' he screamed and began to struggle. They held him tight.

'You can't . . .'

He looked at the ghastly device, with its great iron frame that reached up to the ceiling, and levers and wires, and the board where they laid the victim and the hole that secured the head, the empty black coffin next to the board, the tin receptacle for the head, and the sharp slanting blade that perched at the top of the frame.

His senses swirling, Alex fell into muffled darkness. He came to with a stinging sensation on his face. One of the men was slapping him repeatedly.

'Take a look, 254,' he said. 'This is where your disloyalty will lead you.'

Alex was conscious enough to understand that this was a threat and they were not actually going to execute him.

They turned round and dragged him out of the building. As soon as they were outside the two guards holding on to him let go. Alex's legs gave way and he collapsed on the floor and began to retch. He had yet to eat his breakfast but somewhere from the depths of his stomach he managed to throw up. The bile at the back of his throat tasted horribly bitter.

'*Schweine*,' he croaked, between great gasping sobs. 'How could you be so cruel?'

'Prisoner 254,' said the sergeant, 'you have used disrespectful language towards your guardians. If you utter another word, you will be returned to solitary confinement.'

They untied him and took him back to his cell. By 10.00

145

that morning he had been given back his own clothes and issued with a one-way tram ticket to Treptower Park. As he left, an officer assured him he was looking at several years in a *Jugendwerkhof* – the special prisons for youth offenders – if he came to their attention again.

CHAPTER 20

Every one has secrets but Erich Kohl's were darker than most. Kohl had been a Nazi who started his police career with the Gestapo. Low-level work, flushing out Jews from attics and basements in Berlin and on the northern escape route to Sweden. It was easy work, although his colleague Verner Schluter had got himself into a fine old mess one day in August 1943. Kohl never took chances after that. Why bring them in alive, he told himself, if they were going to kill them anyway?

Kohl knew at least one other Gestapo man like him – Karl Loewe. He had reached a high level in the Stasi. But they never spoke to each other – never even acknowledged each other in the corridor. It was too dangerous, even the slightest connection might put them at risk. Loewe had disappeared a couple of years ago. A casual enquiry as to his whereabouts was met with a brusque 'Comrade Major Loewe is no longer with us.' It was a euphemism they often used when talking about associates who had been executed.

When the Russians arrived, they had killed anyone they suspected of belonging to the Nazi party, the SS and

Gestapo. The SS men had been especially easy to uncover. They all had their blood group tattooed close to the armpit of the left arm. If they were lucky, they were shot on the spot when the Soviets caught up with them. Kohl had seen one SS officer crucified on a wooden door. Thank heavens he hadn't been one of them.

After a few weeks of bloodletting, the Russians began to reconsider. They had a country to run and they needed help. If they killed everyone who was a Nazi, there wouldn't be anyone useful left. Even a few Gestapo men, after a year or two in one of the old Nazi death camps the Soviets had commandeered, were allowed to rejoin the security services. You could usually tell them by the haunted look on their gaunt faces, and the false teeth – ill-fitting steel replacements for those knocked out during 'heightened interrogation'. But you could never tell, even now, what would happen if they discovered you were Gestapo. It was dependent on the whim of your commanding officer.

Kohl had known, as soon as it became obvious the war was lost, that he would have to keep his previous occupation secret. As the Russians closed in on Berlin he used all the skills and guile he had developed over six years in the secret police to fashion a false identity. He'd been Erich Kohl so long now he'd almost forgotten he had been born Gunter Schneider.

Erich Kohl was a policeman. Schneider had found him in the aftermath of an air raid in March 1945. As a match for height and build he was close enough. Kohl was a blast victim – there was barely a mark on him save for bleeding from the ears. Schneider removed the uniform and the identification papers and left the body to be found by the burial parties. What they would make of the young man in his shirtsleeves with no papers and missing trousers, he didn't care. He traced the records a week later and was pleased to notice Kohl had been reported missing. Schneider removed the reference in the file and destroyed it. Then he replaced the photograph on Kohl's pass with one of his own. Getting the correct stamp was easy enough if you knew the right people.

Just before the Russians arrived Schneider's last act at his Gestapo HQ was to take out his own papers and stamp 'DECEASED' on them. He would trace his mother – if she survived all this – and let her know he was OK after everything had died down.

Then he put on Kohl's uniform and was born again. The Soviets were happy to make use of a German policeman who was not a Nazi Party member. Someone had to keep law and order on the streets. Once or twice in the early years he'd let himself down, when people had addressed him by his new name, and he had not responded. But he had been Erich Kohl for so long now he had grown into his skin.

Yet sometimes, when he half heard car doors slam outside his apartment in the middle of the night, or shuffling in the hall on the other side of his front door, he would wake with a start, cold with sweat. Maybe one day they would take him to one of those whitewashed cellar rooms at Normannenstrasse where he had tied prisoners to chairs in front of rows of sandbags and shot them. He knew exactly what to expect.

CHAPTER 21

Geli was at home watching a newsflash on West German television. The Red Army Faction had set off a bomb at a US army base in Heidelberg. Geli felt sick for the people who had been blown to shreds as they went about their ordinary everyday business.

There was the sound of a key in the door. She leapt to her feet and barely recognised the crop-haired urchin standing in the hall.

'We've been so worried,' she said as she hugged Alex tight. 'Sophie came round as soon as she was released. They let her out the next morning and she caught me in at lunchtime, and told us what had happened. Mutti and Vati were furious when they stopped being worried sick about where you were. They'd gone to the police the previous night to report you missing and we were up all night fretting about what had happened to you. You can imagine. Vati even went round to the Kirschs but no one would answer the door.'

Alex sat there too bewildered to reply. The Stasi had not even told his parents he was being held. No doubt they'd be livid with him now they knew what had happened.

Frank and Gretchen were both at work, so Geli went to phone them from the public telephone box at the end of the street. When she came back, Alex was sitting in exactly the same place she had left him. He looked stunned – like an animal caught in the road by approaching headlights.

She couldn't believe what they had done to him. 'I know they're bastards,' she spat, 'but that stunt with the guillotine, that's unbelievable.'

'They wouldn't really, would they?' said Alex.

'I don't know,' said Geli. 'They've done enough terrible things in the past.'

'What happened to Sophie?' he asked.

'I think she got off with a slapped wrist,' said Geli. 'You were the one they were after. Sophie's been worried sick.'

'I'll see her this afternoon,' said Alex suddenly. 'I'll catch her on the way back from school. I can't go round to the Grims after this.'

Geli remembered something. 'There's a letter arrived for you – stamped district housing office.'

Alex tore it open. It was from Herr Kalb. The tone was very formal. The summer job was no longer available.

Alex waited in the park. He felt too unsettled to sit on a bench, so he paced up and down along the path they usually followed on the way back from school. Kalb had been his one hope of avoiding military service. He'd really messed that up.

Alex felt very conspicuous out there on his own. He watched the other people in the park with a wary eye. Were any of the distant figures familiar? Were they watching him?

Sophie was almost standing next to him before he realised she was there. She hugged him and cried. 'What sort of a mess have we got ourselves into?' she said, drying her tears on her sleeve. She composed herself and tried to be cheerful.

'Whooo,' she pointed at his head. 'Now there's a haircut my Vati would approve of.'

She looked around. 'I can't stay long, Alex. Mutter and Vater said I was to come straight home after school. Perhaps you could just walk me home?'

'How was it at school?' said Alex. 'Did anyone say anything?'

'No one knows, yet. I certainly wasn't going to tell them. But it's bound to get out sometime.'

It was an overcast summer afternoon and as they wandered through the fronds and tendrils of an overgrown area of the park, Sophie held Alex's hand as tightly as an anxious child. Conversation was awkward. He wondered whether to tell her about the guillotine then decided against it. It would just make her worry more.

'What did they do to you?' asked Alex.

She looked away.

'They kept telling me you'd told them it was all my

fault,' she said. 'That I'd asked you to come to work with me so we could steal from the canteen cash register.'

Alex laughed. 'They did something similar with me. Told me you'd said I'd bullied you into getting me into the building. Then they accused me of spying. I told them I just wanted to spend some time with you because your parents hated me and never let us see each other.'

Sophie's eyes shot up. 'Well, it's true. They never said anything like that to me, and I never thought to say it.' She looked worried. 'So what have they got in store for us next?'

'I don't care,' said Alex with a defiance he didn't really feel. He wanted Sophie to think the Stasi were not going to intimidate him. Her eyes shone with admiration.

'They got bored with me pretty quickly,' said Sophie. 'Let me out by nine o'clock that evening. Vati was furious, of course. All the neighbours staring out of the window, wondering what I'd been up to. "They probably thought you were streetwalking," he said, "in that ridiculous mini skirt."' She mimicked him cruelly.

They both sniggered. Alex loved it when she was rude about her father.

'And what about your Mutti?'

'Oh, floods of tears. You can imagine.'

'Thank you for coming round to tell my family,' said Alex.

'I went as soon as they released me,' she said.

Alex returned home to face his parents. His father was

white with anxiety and anger. He could barely speak. Alex thought he was going to explode at any moment. His mother looked utterly disconsolate. She gave him a hug, at least, when she saw him, but neither of them could bring themselves to discuss what had happened. Alex could hardly bear to be around them. It was like being with people who had suffered a crushing bereavement.

He went to bed but couldn't sleep. Quite apart from the horrible events of the last couple of days, there was something about Sophie's story that didn't add up. Had they got her too? Was she spying on him now?

CHAPTER 22

Two days later, Alex was walking home from school through the park. It had not been a good day. No one would talk to him in the school yard and his teachers were treating him with icy disdain. Even Sophie was keeping her distance at school, although she still walked there and back with him. That afternoon she had stayed behind for an orchestra rehearsal.

Lost in thought he was startled to be approached by a middle-aged man with greasy black hair, who offered to buy him a cup of coffee. 'Get lost,' said Alex under his breath and quickened his pace. He wondered whether to run for it. The fellow might be old but he looked pretty tough.

The man looked weary rather than angry. He took out an identity card and flashed it under Alex's nose. 'Erich Kohl. State Security. We'll forget the coffee. You can just sit here on this park bench.'

Alex's heart was beating hard and his mind was reeling. What had they discovered now? Were they going to take him back to Hohenschönhausen?

'This has not been a promising start to our

conversation, Alex Ostermann,' he said. 'Let us try to be civil from now on, shall we?'

Alex said nothing. But his fear ebbed a little. Perhaps he wasn't about to be arrested after all.

'You have been a great disappointment to your country,' said the man. 'You have made things very awkward for yourself and now you have a difficult future. You are currently one step away from the *Jugendwerkhof*. But you can make amends by helping us.'

Alex stared ahead as his anxiety turned to frustration. He knew exactly where this was going.

'We will assist you in your attempt to further your education, but, in turn, you must agree to tell us about the behaviour of your fellow students – anything that strikes you as outside the norm . . .' Kohl let his words sink in. 'We will even pay you a reasonable sum to help you with your studies.'

Alex tried hard to think of a suitable response. His first instinct was to be rude – but he knew that would get him nowhere. Now he was feeling cornered and there was a terrible anxiety rising in his chest. He played for time.

'You are asking me to do something I have never considered before. I would like to be able to think this through.'

'Very well,' said the man. 'Think on it. We are asking you to provide a valuable and honourable service to the State. I will contact you again shortly.'

The man got up abruptly, leaving Alex to sit on the

bench in an anxious daze. So this was what they had in store for him. All at once, there in the great wide spaces of the park, he felt trapped, almost as if he was locked in a little cupboard or nailed into a coffin.

Two envelopes lay on the doormat when Alex returned home. Both were addressed to Frank Ostermann. Geli was there too and she and Alex could guess what they were. They wondered whether or not to throw them away.

'He's got to find out one of these days,' said Geli.

Alex shrugged. 'When you've been threatened with the guillotine, a scolding from Mutti and Vati doesn't register as much of an ordeal.'

Frank opened the letters as soon as he got home. Gretchen poured him a whisky. He drained the glass in a single gulp and sat on his chair staring straight ahead.

'You'll have a seizure, *mein Schatz*,' said Gretchen and stroked his head. Then she turned to Alex and Geli. 'See what you've done to your father.'

They both looked down.

'Both of you rejected from your further education,' said Gretchen. 'What is this? Some kind of infection?'

She tried to maintain a pretence of anger but she could not keep it up. She was fighting back tears now. 'It's my fault, I suppose. I always encouraged you with your art and your music. And you were always so keen. Neither of you have your father's head for mathematics. It's a shame you didn't take after Frank and study electronics. The State welcomes creative thinking in the field of engineering. How unfortunate that you were born into a world where art and music must follow Party guidelines you both chose to disregard. Well, we are all paying for that now.'

Frank spoke in a low, angry voice. 'I should never have allowed you to follow these two pursuits. I should never have permitted you to waste your talents on . . . *guitar*,' he spat out the word. 'You should have done something more acceptable, like trumpet or trombone. But you always had a frivolous streak, didn't you, Alex? You always had a vanity.'

He turned to Geli. 'And you – we expected more from you. You had such drive and dedication. You were so determined. I wish I had never given you a camera.'

Geli was getting angry. 'You are deceiving yourself, Vater. I only show the truth. Do you want me to go down to Alexanderplatz and make it look warm and vibrant . . . like they try to do on that stupid TV show? It's a soulless place, just like this whole country.'

She stopped to gather her thoughts. No one said a word. 'Just look at this apartment . . . this ordinary every-day building . . . It has elegance. Look at the windows and curves and lines . . .' She opened up the curtain overlooking the street. 'Look at our beautiful balcony . . .' It had wrought-iron railings fashioned as intertwining leaves, in a russet-red art nouveau style.

'Why could they do this seventy years ago and not now? It's the same country. Do you think people will look back on Honecker's buildings and think they're beautiful?'

Frank would not look at her. 'I have tolerated your false opinions long enough,' he said in a flat, low voice. 'Your consciousness is corrupted.' He gestured towards the balcony railing. 'Bourgeois art, made by good working-class craftsmen . . . exploited by capitalists for a pittance.'

Geli spoke plainly, trying to keep the anger from her voice. 'So why can't the State encourage our craftsmen to make beautiful things and pay them proper wages? Everything here is ugly and joyless. Grey concrete, brown lino, green curtains. The same outfits for everyone – almost like in China. Why do you think Alex and I love the Western fashions so much? They are attractive and lively and say life should be fun. I'm sick of trying to be a good socialist robot.'

A terrible silence fell on the room. Alex was spellbound in admiration for his sister. She had put his feelings into words.

'Angela, half the country was destroyed in the war,' said Frank. 'It is still being rebuilt. Why do I need to tell you this?'

'The war ended nearly thirty years ago,' said Geli.

'Angela, go to your room,' said Gretchen. 'No, both of you go.' She was close to tears. Their father looked like a wounded animal.

It was the dreariest June any of them could remember. Berlin was covered in a perpetual grey sky – like someone had sealed the city in a vast plastic food container. The wind blew in from the East and it seemed impossible to believe summer would ever arrive. The atmosphere in the Ostermann household was very similar.

Alex felt a terrible inertia – he had real problems getting out of bed. His future – one he could imagine actually looking forward to and enjoying – had been taken away from him. Sophie was the only bright spark in his life, and he wondered how much longer she would want to go out with a lad who had such dismal prospects. Alex even began to wonder if he should play along with the Stasi – pretend to spy for them and deliver nothing of any value. But he sensed they were too clever, too ruthless, to let him get away with that.

Frank shouted at everyone these days – even Gretchen moved around him with trepidation, anxious not to set him off on a rant. So when they sat down for dinner that night, no one was looking forward to the stop-start conversations that characterised their meals these days.

'I have an announcement to make,' said Frank, after he had drunk a glass of the Bulgarian wine that occasionally appeared on the shelves of the local supermarket. 'I have been thinking a lot about our life together, and I think we'd all agree it is not satisfactory.'

Geli and Alex looked at him in horror. What was he about to say? That he and Gretchen were getting divorced?

His next words were even more of a shock.

'I think we should try to leave the DDR.'

Geli's jaw dropped open. Gretchen looked astonished. Alex couldn't believe what he was hearing.

'There is nothing left for us here. Your mother and I are shunned by our Party comrades.' He reached over to hold her hand. 'You two have destroyed the future we worked so hard to prepare you for . . .'

Alex could see Geli bristling with anger. He hoped she wouldn't say anything.

Gretchen spoke. 'But, Frank, you know those who register to leave are treated as traitors. They'll never let us go. They're always saying how important engineers and teachers are to the future of our country. We are exactly the sort of people they would never allow to leave.'

Frank nodded. He looked grave. 'That is why I have engaged the services of professionals.'

'You mean lawyers,' said Gretchen. 'They won't do any good and they'll cost us a fortune.'

'I mean professional escape assistants.'

There was a stunned silence around the table.

Eventually their mother said, 'How do you know people like that?' She was utterly astonished. Frank had spent his whole life associating with people who were loyal to the Party.

'I have contacts at work. I hope you will understand that it is not expedient to discuss this further. Please. You must trust me. I will tell you more when our mode of operations is clear.'

'No, tell us now,' said Gretchen. 'I need to know that these people aren't going to be the death of us.'

'You mean you're not going to object,' said Alex to his mother. He couldn't believe what he was hearing.

'What am I going to do?' she said angrily. 'Stay here on my own? We've tried to make our life here as a family. We've failed. If you're all going, I'm not going to stop you and I am certainly not going to be left behind.' She looked at Frank sternly. 'Now tell us. Who are these people?'

Frank gathered his thoughts.

'They are business people. They bring goods over from West Berlin – luxury stuff for the *Exquisit* and *Delikat* stores, and on the way back they take export goods from the East. All the kinds of things we make that have a market in the West – *Praktika* cameras, Meissen porcelain. Two of the drivers run their own little business taking people back to the West. It is a well-worn routine – the guards know them by sight now and they are usually just waved through. And if they do stop and search the lorries they have the people in a really good hiding place – false compartments and all that.'

'So we'd have to leave everything behind,' said Gretchen. 'I can't imagine we'd be allowed to bring anything more than a little bag and the clothes we stand up in.'

She put a hand on Frank's wrist. 'Look at this apartment. We were really lucky to get it. Geli is right. It is beautiful – especially compared to the ones they're

163

putting up these days. Do you really want to leave this behind?'

Geli didn't like the way the conversation was going. 'Mutti – there's nothing left for us here – Vati is right. In the West we can make use of our talents. You will be able to get a job – teachers are never out of work. Vati is always going to find work with his skills. Alex will be able to play his music without the Stasi hauling him off to Hohenschönhausen. I'd go tomorrow with just the clothes I stand up in, if I had the chance.'

Gretchen was looking tearful. 'But what about Jan-Carl?' she asked Geli. She turned to Frank. 'What about Grandma?'

'She can come and visit us as often as she likes. They'd even let her go if she wanted to move to the West, you know that.'

Geli spoke next. 'I'll miss Jan-Carl,' she said plainly, 'but we were never going to get married or anything.'

'And you, Alex,' said Gretchen. 'What about Sophie? What about your friends?'

'She'll follow us out,' said Alex. 'When I tell her, she'll be desperate to come with us.' His eyes lit up. 'Can she come with us?'

'No, no. You must tell no one,' Frank shouted. He looked terrified. 'Sophie might want to escape, but you must swear on your life that you will not tell her,' he said. 'I know it's difficult but if no one knows, then no one will be able to tell anyone else. Any stray gossip will be the

164

end for us. We simply cannot tell a soul that we are going. Not even Grandma.'

'So when will we go?' said Gretchen.

'There's a space for us next week,' said Frank.

'NEXT WEEK!' said Gretchen. 'You are joking. We'll never be ready for next week.'

'Gretchen, my love,' said Frank. 'This is not like going on holiday. We do not have to get the neighbours in to water the plants and make sure the gas bill is paid and our workmates are covering our absences. We have all got to drop everything.'

Even Alex and Geli were stunned at the implication.

'And how are we going to pay for it?' asked Gretchen.

'There's been a cancellation,' said Frank. 'That's why it's at such short notice. They said they'd do the four of us for a bargain price. We've been saving for a fridge, Mutti and me – and you know how expensive they are – so we've got just enough money.'

That night, each one of them sat in their rooms looking at a lifetime's worth of possessions – their own little treasures. In his head Alex knew he wanted to go, but in his heart he felt empty. He decided he would have to take his little plastic Sandman, that he had loved so much as a kid. And a few clothes. But he'd have to leave his guitar. He loved that – even though he knew it was crap. It was the repository of his dreams.

Geli looked at all her art books and sketches and photo prints, all carefully archived and the fruit of so much labour. Years of going out at all hours to take shots in exactly the right light. She went through her negative files, picking out the pictures she could not bear to leave behind and cut them out with scissors.

Gretchen was looking at photographs too – in the bulky family albums that filled an entire shelf above the television. She had a whole life in those photographs – how could she possibly choose just a handful of shots of the kids when they were younger? Then she thought about all her carefully acquired kitchenware, and how hard they had worked to scrape together enough money for the washing machine and the cooker and the food mixer.

Frank was thinking of the Trabi – all the tender love and affection he had put into keeping it on the road. He thought back to their first family outing and how much it had meant to them to be able to tootle out to the lakes east of Berlin without having to wait for trams and trains and buses with arms full of food hampers and blankets and towels. Everything in their life they had had to struggle and strive to get. And now, they were leaving it all behind.

CHAPTER 23

The escape was set for 1st of July, in the dead of night, and now the waiting was almost over. For Alex, it would not be soon enough. Not having Sophie would leave a huge gap, but his day to day life in the Republik was now so restricted, he felt he was being slowly suffocated. These days he only ventured out when he had to – the walk to school and back. He was sure he was being followed. He kept waiting for the moment when Kohl would tap him on the shoulder and ask if he had decided to help them.

Two days before they were due to go, Frank told them they were to meet the escape assistants at 10 p.m. in a bar close to the Meissen warehouse. Having spent so long deciding what to take, word had come down that they could only carry handbags or small rucksacks. 'Think about it,' said Frank's contact. 'A family all carrying suitcases would raise suspicion. You might even get stopped in the street by the police.' That upset them all. The escape itself was bad enough – like taking a leap into a dark well with no guarantee that there would be any water at the bottom.

Frank made it plain to Alex that he should not spend

his final evening with Sophie. He was too anxious that the boy would tell her he was going to escape. Alex was furious. 'You have got to trust me, Vati,' he said. 'I, more than any of us, am desperate to get out of this place. Why would I place the entire family in danger?'

Gretchen had said, 'You should do what Geli did with Jan-Carl and tell her it's over. He was civil enough about it.'

Alex told them he would think about it. But every time he meant to tell her when they met up on the way to school, he'd look at her face and the way she looked at him and he couldn't bear to think they'd never talk to each other, or kiss, or walk in the park again. In the back of his mind, he knew they wouldn't be able to do any of these things after he escaped. But there was something so frightening about what they were about to do, it seemed to eclipse everything in the future.

Frank and Gretchen relented. They allowed Alex to go out the night before, to see Sophie one last time. Maybe Kohl only worked during the day, Alex convinced himself. And even if he did nab him, Alex could agree to anything he asked. He wouldn't be there after tomorrow.

She met him in the park in floods of tears. Alex was immediately alarmed. How did she know?

But something else was upsetting her.

'My father is so angry with me for going out to see you tonight,' she said. '"You're a big girl now, so you have to make your own stupid mistakes," he said. "If you keep seeing Alex Ostermann, you are putting your entire future in peril.'"

Alex said nothing. Her father was right.

They walked along to the Soviet war memorial and then to the fair. They were both short of money and decided they would rather spend their few Marks on something to drink rather than another ride on the Ferris wheel.

They sat on a bench and watched the wheel go round. It was a bizarre situation and every moment Alex was bursting to tell her what he was about to do.

Eventually, when the beer bottles were empty, he could bear it no longer.

'Sophie, I'm going to tell you something you must promise never to repeat to anyone else.'

She looked at him with trepidation.

'I'm going to escape. Tomorrow night. We're all going.'

'All,' she said, her eyes widening with shocked surprise. 'You mean me as well?'

'No – I mean the family.'

'Alex, how could you do this without telling me about it?' She had raised her voice in anger. 'You know I want to go. Why have you done this behind my back?'

'It's something my parents have organised. Yes, I'm as surprised as you are about it. Of course I asked if you could come too, but they said there was only room for the four of us.'

He looked at her angry face and wished he'd had the good sense to keep his mouth shut.

'They made me promise not to tell a soul,' he pleaded. 'Look, you can imagine how difficult it's been.'

'*Verdammt*, Alex, you *Arschloch*,' she said, and slapped him hard across the face.

Before he could gather his thoughts she had got up and was storming off home. He called out but people were already staring at them. Alex got up to chase after her. But she was walking so quickly and so determinedly he knew he was wasting his time.

CHAPTER 24

For Alex, the final hours passed slower than a day in his cell at Hohenschönhausen. In its own strange way, he imagined it would be like the last day before your execution. Almost everything he knew would be gone for ever. The only thing the Ostermanns would be keeping from their previous life was their grandma. Alex didn't know what she would think about them escaping. Perhaps she'd feel they had abandoned her and fret about not having them close by in case she got ill and needed help. But once they'd settled there, she could come out and join them.

Alex sat in his room, filled with a sadness he did not really understand. Perhaps life would have been easier if he'd just kept his head down and gone along with it all? Sorting through his things he found a small box with all his enamel Young Pioneer badges, glistening gold and red, and thought how proud he'd been to receive them.

In her bedroom next door Geli was looking at her *Jugendweihe* collection – the youth coming of age ceremony she had been through when she was fourteen. She had no scruples about leaving any of it behind. She told herself the most precious thing she had was her talent. Over there, in the West, it would be allowed to flourish.

As the shadows deepened and the bright light of the day began to fade, Gretchen cooked them a final meal of roast pork and dumplings.

'Why make all that washing-up?' Frank demanded.

'Why do we need to do the washing-up?' she replied.

They were all shocked by that. In all his sixteen years, Alex had never seen their mother leave the dishes after a meal.

In the end Gretchen couldn't bear to leave the kitchen looking so untidy. 'It's not fair to whoever comes to live here next,' she said. Geli and Alex helped her wash and dry the dishes. It helped to take their mind off what was coming.

Then they gathered up whatever they could carry in their coats and small bags.

'Have you remembered the money?' Alex said, almost as a joke.

Frank never had much of a sense of humour at the best of times. 'I have paid them already.'

Walking out of their home for the last time felt like a strange dream. Frank locked the door behind them and they began to walk down the stairs. Then he went back to unlock the door and leave the keys on the kitchen table. He did not want the authorities to have to break into the apartment. A damaged door would be a needless expense.

The tram stop out to their rendezvous point – Waldes Bar on the corner of Baumschulenstrasse and Kiefholzstrasse and close to the crossing point at Sonnenallee – was a five minute walk from the apartment.

As they waited silently for their tram, Alex thought about a lesson they'd had in school about escapers to the West and what life was like there. It was an act of political and moral depravity, his teacher had said.

Bollocks to that, he thought defiantly. But he had never felt such a mixture of emotions in his life. Sadness that he and Sophie had parted so badly, fear for the ordeal they now faced, excitement for the future, but also a strange nostalgia for the life he was just about to leave behind. It was all he had ever known and now he might never see these streets again.

The Waldes Bar was as seedy as expected, with a few desultory customers and dim light bulbs. Everyone turned to look at them when they walked in. But none of the customers looked especially threatening.

A waitress came to the table and took their order – two small beers and two orange juices.

'Now we wait for them to come to us,' said Frank.

They sat down in glum silence and Alex wondered if they ought to be talking. Why would a family of four be sitting in this bar at ten o'clock at night, just waiting? It all looked too suspicious. They should pretend they had just been to see a film or a play or a concert – anything like that. They should be talking in an animated way rather than sitting there like they were just about to have a tooth out at the dentist.

Five minutes after they'd ordered drinks a stocky middle-aged man in a sheepskin driving coat came into the bar and approached them.

'Ah, Frank,' he said. 'I understand you want to buy my refrigerator.'

Frank answered as agreed. 'Yes, you need a refrigerator at this time of year.'

'Come along then, I'll show it to you.'

They got up as casually as possible, and followed him out, leaving their drinks unfinished. As Geli squeezed past a narrow gap between tables she dropped the photo file she was carrying inside her coat and its contents spilled out over the floor.

'Leave them,' snapped Frank and everyone in the bar looked over. The expression on Geli's face told them she was about to lash out at him in her anger.

'Here, I'll help you,' said Gretchen, and they quickly gathered up the negatives and prints. As they left, one or two of the customers were still eyeing them warily.

'You took your time,' said the man waiting outside. The wait had unnerved him. 'You need to get a move on. Go quickly to 35 Frauenlobstrasse, it's two blocks away on the left. Knock on the door. They are expecting you. I will be there in a few minutes.' He hurried off in the opposite direction.

Frank tried to rally his frightened family. 'In an hour's time,' he said with an enthusiasm he didn't feel, 'this will all be over!'

They walked along, their footsteps echoing about the deserted street. Alex's eyes darted around. Anyone they saw out here now might be coming to arrest them. Although the street was empty, that did not stop him wondering who might be watching them from the dark corners and doorways.

CHAPTER 25

As they approached the house in Frauenlobstrasse, Alex could see the glow of a cigarette in the dark recess of the doorway. A man emerged as they approached. No words of introduction were spoken. He merely said, 'Follow me,' and took them to a warehouse just around the corner, where they were hurried in through a small door at the rear. In the dim light they could see hundreds of boxes of Meissen porcelain, all waiting to be packed. There was no one about.

Their means of escape stood before them – a big Mercedes four-wheeler with a separate driver's compartment and a large cargo container with rear-opening doors. The workmen were away having a short coffee break, before they began to load the lorry.

'You're late,' their driver fretted. 'We need to hurry.'

Alex had one final thought before he boarded the lorry. Holger had once told him people paid huge sums of money to professional escape assistants to get them out – like 10,000 Marks or more. Frank had told his family these people were taking them for 1,000. This wasn't right. It was a fraction of what it usually cost. Alex keep that thought to himself. It was too late now. He felt strangely detached from everything that was happening, almost like he was watching himself in a dream and had no control over what he was going to do next.

There was a little compartment right at the front of the container – like a false bottom on a suitcase, only upright and stretching from the floor to the ceiling.

'Good thing none of you are fat,' said the driver brusquely. There was just enough space for the four of them, if they put their little bags between their feet and squashed up shoulder to shoulder.

The compartment door clicked into place and they were left in darkness.

'I hope we can breathe OK here,' said Gretchen.

'No talking,' said the driver from the other side of the door.

Now the Ostermanns lived in a world of sound. Alex could feel his heart beating hard in his chest. He tried to breathe deeply to control his mounting apprehension. Then he worried if he would be using up too much air. Surely there would be a vent built into the compartment?

A couple of minutes later they heard loud voices and the lorry rocked a little on its chassis. They could hear boots thumping and scraping on the floor of the cargo compartment. There were scuffling and knocking sounds right next to the false wall as the men loaded the boxes of cargo into the lorry. Alex reached over to Geli and squeezed her hand. He tried to suppress a tingling in his nose that was making him want to sneeze.

The banging and scuffling went on for about ten minutes, gradually receding as the lorry filled from front to back. Alex was desperate to pinch his nose, or blow it – something to stop the sneeze he could feel building up. But the space they were in was so confined he couldn't move his hands up to his face.

He started to breathe deeply to try to make it go away, but all of a sudden it exploded out of him. A voice at the back of the lorry shouted, 'Stop your loading. Wait a minute.'

There were footsteps around the lorry and a banging on the passenger door. 'I heard someone sneeze inside the lorry,' said the voice. Alex sensed fear run between the four of them like an electric current.

Someone in the driver's cab – it sounded like the man who had met them in the bar – said, 'You did. It was me.'

'No,' said the man. He sounded angry. 'It was inside the lorry.'

Another voice inside the cab said, 'It was Heinz.' He laughed in a good-natured way. 'I was sitting right next to him.'

There was a long silence. Then the loading continued. The rear doors slammed shut.

'Now we're going,' whispered Frank.

But they didn't. They waited for an age. 'Do you think the one who heard me has gone to get someone?' whispered Alex. A couple of short knocks came from the driver's cab to tell them to shut up.

The engine spluttered into life and the whole vehicle

began to vibrate and tremble. 'Off you go,' someone shouted and they were buffeted to and fro as the vehicle turned into the street. It was disconcerting, feeling motion that you could not see. Alex began to feel a little nauseous – and prayed he would not be sick.

The journey to the checkpoint at Sonnenallee was mercifully brief. There was very little traffic at that time of night. Within five minutes the lorry engine stopped again. The driver and border guards exchanged pleasantries. Their voices were so close Alex felt as if he was standing next to them. In the silence he worried that even their breathing would give them away. Every exhalation, every sniff, seemed dangerously loud. Looking at the ceiling Alex could see the odd cracks of light through the joints in the frame of the container and realised they must be under intensely bright lighting. Seeing these little dots and beams gave him some comfort. If light could get in, so could air.

The engine burst into life again, sending a tremor through the whole vehicle. Alex had to bite his lip to stop himself cheering. They were on their way. He tried to picture the scene outside. The lorry moving between the flat open ground of the checkpoint and on towards the Western barrier under heavy arc lamps that cast stark black shadows. In a few seconds they would be there on the other side.

Someone was shouting. What was being said over the noise of the engine was impossible to hear. A sudden rattle of machine-gun fire made them all flinch and try to make their bodies smaller – but there was no space to crouch.

Alex heard Gretchen stifle a terrified scream. They stood stiff and upright in their little space, feeling intensely vulnerable. The next few seconds would decide their fate.

The lorry stopped with a squeal of brakes and rattle of crockery. There was more shouting. A cabin door creaked open and slammed. The driver yelled at the border guards in an angry, panicky voice.

Then there were more shots. A man screamed in pain. The lorry shook a little as the other driver got out and there was the sound of running. A further burst of machine-gun fire followed and a shattering of porcelain as a stray bullet penetrated the cargo hold close to where they stood. Alex was so frightened it took a supreme effort of will not to wet himself.

There was silence, then, again, the sound of running boots on tarmac.

Voices came over from the Western side. And footsteps. A heated exchange – a man explaining forcibly that the lorry was on the Western side of the border now and they were going to take it further. Then there were other voices. A guard explaining that the drivers had brandished guns and threatened them. That was why they had opened fire from the East, he said.

Even in their dark world Alex could not believe that.

Another voice, he guessed from the East, declared that they had challenged the lorry drivers, when word came through just as they were leaving the checkpoint. The vehicle, they were told, contained contraband.

The Western guard was getting angry. He was a high ranking officer, he explained, and the lorry was now on the Western side. They would search it thoroughly and inform the East German guards if the lorry was carrying anything illegal. Much to Alex's surprise and relief, the Eastern guards accepted this without another word.

The lorry rocked a little as someone climbed into the cab. The engine started and they drove on for a short while. When they stopped, Frank and Gretchen began calling out for help. It took fifteen minutes for the lorry to be emptied sufficiently for the compartment to be opened. The door slid open and they were confronted by three men peering at them with anxious faces. Although he expected as much, it was a huge relief for Alex to see they were wearing the uniform of the West German Federal Defence Force.

Frank managed a startled grin. '*Guten Tag!*' he said and put out his hand. 'Thank you for rescuing us.'

Alex staggered out into the cold night air and bright lights that hurt his eyes. They were on the edge of the border crossing – it stretched back to the Eastern side, all flat concrete road, wide open on all sides. Over in the distant Eastern checkpoint buildings there was no one to be seen.

He was drenched in sweat and immediately began to shiver. Four West German guards were walking towards them with two stretchers. The bodies they carried were both covered by blankets. Alex turned his back on his family and was violently sick.

CHAPTER 26

Colonel Theissen had let his routine paperwork slip of late. His department had been deluged with work concerning the forthcoming Olympics and the political reliability of the athletes who would travel to Munich. Theissen was irritated by this. These people had had the best their country could offer. Why would they sacrifice their futures when they stood on the threshold of Olympic triumph? A few of them, especially the younger ones, were exhibiting an aggressive rebelliousness. If there were defections, heads would roll.

After several days of assessing the athletes' profiles it was with some relief he turned to more mundane matters. Kohl's latest report was at the top of his pile. As was common practice with Western operations, the report subjects were now identified by codenames:

```
The operation to infiltrate LATCH, KEY,
BOLT and LOCK, into West Berlin, executed
in conjunction with CENTRAL EVALUATION
AND INFORMATION GROUP and DIRECTORATE
XVI, has been successful.
```

It also gave us the opportunity to carry
out preventative action in the struggle
against anti-State trade in border
violators. During operation, on night of
1st/2nd July, two professional human
traffickers were liquidated. Previously
discharged small arms carefully placed on
bodies of ALBERT METZGER and HEINZ AMSEL
to back up our defence that our border
guards returned fire as self-protection
measure.

LATCH ordered to report on weekly basis
to Western Sector operative 122.

Theissen smiled to himself. Kohl had done well organis-
ing this action in such a short time. He had handled
the last-minute change in the operation from counter-
subversive surveillance to espionage in a very satisfactory
manner. The idea of despatching the human traffickers
was his too – a perfect opportunity. Theissen wondered if
it was time to reassign Kohl to Western operations. Of
course it was. Just as long as they kept him away from the
Red Army Faction. He was certainly the right man for
this particular endeavour. Theissen picked up his telephone and called Kohl into his office.

CHAPTER 27

The first week passed in a daze. The shooting left Alex in a state of shock and the whole experience of being in the West was completely overwhelming. There was so much to take in. So much that was different.

Most things in the West smelled nice – it was one of the first things Alex noticed. The shops, the clothes, the people. It wasn't that the East smelled bad. But here, people wore perfume or aftershave, they did their laundry in washing powder that gave a nice scent. Scent was a bourgeois indulgence you didn't find in East German domestic products.

The authorities took good care of the Ostermanns: within a few days they had moved from a temporary hostel into a first-floor apartment close to Pankstrasse U-Bahn. Alex was astonished to be provided with such a fine new home, and so quickly. This one overlooked recently built government offices and was one of a series of apartment blocks that lined the street. The rooms were huge, with great high ceilings, and Geli and Alex had a bedroom each. Everything about the place was a constant delight. When they first arrived, Geli called to Alex, 'Come and look at this!'

She beckoned him over to the bathroom and they peered through the door. 'Hot and cold running water, black and white tiles, a bath AND a shower!' she exclaimed. It was the height of opulence after a lifetime of bathing in the kitchen using a little tin bath and a rubber hose attached to the sink.

And there was central heating. They had that in schools and offices in the East, but not in people's homes. You switched it on at a control panel on the wall and a gas boiler fired up and pumped hot water to radiators placed in every room. 'They tell me it's no more or less expensive than any other kind of heating,' said Frank.

'Imagine that,' said Alex. 'Being warm without having to lug coal up six flights of stairs.'

Alex couldn't believe the shops. The bright lights, the gaudiness, the adverts selling everything from washing powder to luxury motor cars. It was complete sensory overload. In their first week the whole family were taken to the KDW – the biggest and most famous department store in Germany. Here they were reluctantly photographed by the newspapers, keen for a story on the latest escapers from the East enjoying the bountiful fruits of capitalism.

All the goods on display – it was unbelievable. 'Look at this,' Alex said aloud in wonder. 'A whole aisle of fridges and another of washing machines.'

The clothes department astounded them too. 'You could wear a different skirt or dress for every day of the year,' said Geli.

'If you had the money,' said Frank.

The cheap little supermarket at the end of the street had the kind of goods you'd be lucky to find in the expensive *Delikat* stores in the East. Gretchen came back from there with carrier bags full to bursting. 'Three different kinds of tomatoes. Five different kinds of apples. Bananas on the shelves every day of the week, for heaven's sake, rather than once or twice a year.' She was ecstatic.

It seemed that everything was different. Even the toilet paper. You could get it in white or green or pink or blue, and it was *soft*. The stuff in the East was a uniform dingy brown, looked like it was made from straw and sawdust, and was rough enough to scrape paint from a brick wall.

A few days after their escape Geli and Alex went to a café on Prinzenallee. Sitting in the corner sipping Coca-Cola, the preferred beverage of the Number One Class Enemy, they watched a boy come in and put a song on the jukebox. The chorus went on about school being out completely, or something. They didn't quite understand the words but it was so loud and 'negative-decadent' Alex wanted to grab a guitar and play along with it. And here they were in broad daylight, just a short walk away from the nearest police station, listening to it in public and nobody gave a damn. Even some of the police had *long hair* here! Alex was so happy he could cry. He looked at Geli. She had tears in her eyes too.

Alex asked the boy what the record was. He looked at

him as though he was an idiot. 'Alice Cooper,' he sneered and walked off muttering about 'Dumb Ossies'. Alex wondered how the boy had known they were from the East. Maybe it was his prison haircut, which had yet to grow out. He cheered himself up by using all his free change to play the record three times in a row. It was a song they would hear a lot that summer.

The sun was shining brightly so Alex and Geli decided this was the day they would go to look at the Wall. It was a kilometre or two from their apartment and as they approached there was no sense of stepping into a forbidden zone, as there had been in the East. The buildings here were even occupied right to the very edge of the border. Close to the Wall they could see it had been covered from top to bottom, as far as the eye could see, with bold multicoloured graffiti. Oblivious to the stares of passers-by, Geli and Alex burst into hysterical laughter. They really were free.

As they stood there, a summer breeze blew over from the East, carrying a familiar whiff of compressed coal dust and temperamental old boilers. They had never really noticed it when they lived there, but now the smell of it made them both feel a little homesick.

'I wonder what will happen to our apartment?' said Geli wistfully.

Alex, with a mixture of regret and sadness, wondered what Sophie was doing. Somewhere over the Wall they could hear the distant chug of a two-stroke Trabi engine.

* * *

After a couple of weeks Alex began to have terrible dreams about the escape and the two men he had heard being machine-gunned to death. Whenever he thought of it, a wave of nausea passed through him. And in the early hours, as he tried to block the incident from his mind, his thoughts would turn to Sophie. He had told her they were going. Had she tipped off the Stasi? She couldn't have, he told himself. Maybe someone else in his family had told a friend? But he couldn't imagine they had. He reluctantly concluded that it must have been her. Perhaps it was because she was so angry with him when he left. Or perhaps, and this brought a lump to his throat, perhaps she had been reporting on him all along? They seemed to know so much about him – about as much as Sophie herself.

Alex consoled himself by reflecting that at least he wasn't thinking about this in an East German prison cell. With nothing else to do, this sense of nagging guilt and nebulous anger would have gone round and round, eating away at him. It would have driven him insane. Fortunately, now they were here, there was plenty to take his mind off Sophie. He and Geli had begun to meet kids their own age in the streets and cafés around Pankstrasse. The newspaper stories just after their escape granted them a brief celebrity. But this faded quickly enough. With a growing sense of unease, Alex began to realise they were seen as rather quaint.

Part of the problem, Alex understood, was how little

they had in common. Conversations here mystified him, with their references to characters like Asterix and Tintin. They had all read a book called *Lord of the Rings*. He had never heard of it. Nobody knew about his childhood TV heroes, apart from Sandman, and their eyes glazed over when he tried to tell his new acquaintances about them.

Alex and Geli both felt embarrassed about the clothes they had been given when they arrived or hurriedly bought with their refugee grant. Geli, especially, was conscious of the fact that her outfits looked cheap and gaudy compared to the West Berlin girls she was meeting. 'Everything you wear tells the world how chic or dowdy you are, how rich or poor,' she complained. In the East everyone wore five-Mark sneakers – they were all the same. Here you had a bewildering array of footwear. She looked at her hair and make-up and knew instinctively she wasn't getting it right.

And it took a while to get used to people's manners. In the East you always said '*Guten Morgen*' and shook hands. Here, people barely looked at you, said 'Hi', and gave a little wave. They seemed informal to the point of rudeness. And people seemed so much more forceful. If you were in a restaurant in the East and there were four chairs around a table, then four people sat at that table. In the West, if a fifth person arrived, they would take a chair from another table and squeeze in. Sometimes they would not even ask the waiter if they minded. No one would do such a thing in the East. Behaviour like that would be considered brash and outlandish.

As they grew more confident with their new surroundings, Geli and Alex ventured further afield. In maps back in Treptower, West Berlin had been a white blank. It was fascinating to discover the city on the U-Bahn and S-Bahn, underground and overground. All the trains here were electric or diesel – unlike the chugging steam trains of the east. Everything was so modern.

Some of the U-Bahn trains they took ran part of their journey under East Berlin and through the ghost stations. Alex wondered, as they trundled under Alexanderplatz, when they would pass the exact spot where he and Sophie had sat to eat their sausages and feed the sparrows.

Every day there was something new to get excited about. They enjoyed daydreaming as they ogled the windows of travel agents. Pictures of Big Ben, the Eiffel Tower, the Pyramids, and the skyscrapers of New York, filled them with a restless desire to travel. 'We'll get part-time jobs and in no time we'll have enough money to get to London,' Geli assured Alex. 'Then next year, maybe we can all go to New York!'

All these things were possible now, if you had the money. There was no Stasi, or school political officer, or concrete and barbed wire Wall, to prevent you from going.

Geli took a waitressing job. She came home and told them how she had been scolded by the boss for being distant with the customers. 'They don't have to come here,' he told her, 'so smile and make them feel welcome.' Geli laughed about this.

'Why should I smile?' she told her family. 'I've never met these people in my life.'

Alex found a job in the supermarket close to where they lived, stacking shelves. And he helped out at a music shop at weekends. Frank warned him that he would have to pack in one of those jobs when he went back to school in the autumn. But Alex was earning money. If he kept going at this rate, he would soon have enough for a trip to London, or even a Les Paul copy – a cheap Japanese guitar that looked exactly like the one Jimmy Page played. There was one in the shop where he worked. His boss had already told him he would give him a good discount.

One day in the third week of July, Grandma Ostermann came to visit. It had been quite a performance discovering where they lived. Once she had realised they had left, on her next visit to the West she had gone to a police station and explained she was looking for her son. They asked her to return in a few days. By then the Ostermanns had been contacted by the police and arranged to meet her at Sonnenallee.

She was impressed with their apartment and began to wonder if she should move to the West too. Grandma said she would think about it. She still had plenty of friends in Treptower and the government looked after her well enough.

She had brought newspaper reports about the breach

in the Anti-Fascist Protective Barrier and the death of two human traffickers, Albert Metzger and Heinz Amsel, who were both pictured. They had been 'shot whilst trying to escape'. There were no photographs of the Ostermanns, though, and no mention of their name, which Alex thought was a bit odd.

Alex asked whether she had seen Sophie. Grandma looked surprised at his question.

'I thought she might have been round by now, to see if we were all right,' he said.

'No. No sign of her,' said Grandma and swiftly asked Gretchen if she had remembered to get some fruit for her to take back East.

They loaded Grandma's bag with oranges, bananas and chocolate and Gretchen and Frank took the U-Bahn and travelled with her down to Sonnenallee where they had so recently escaped. Alex and Geli refused to go with them – that night still haunted them both.

Frank found West Berlin more difficult than the rest of them. He hated the long hair on the boys and the tiny little mini skirts on the girls, and the way the youth chewed gum. Even the way they walked annoyed him. And he was disturbed by the hollow-eyed girls and boys he had seen around Zoo Station, selling their bodies to middle-aged men. He assumed they were drug addicts and worried that his own children might end up like that.

'Never mind,' said Gretchen to Alex and Geli, after

Frank had delivered a particularly vehement tirade about paper tissues and how wasteful they were compared to handkerchiefs. 'He will get used to it. As soon as he finds a job he will settle and then we can all start enjoying our new life. Alex take Vati out for a walk. Take him window-shopping down Prinzenallee. Remind him what he can buy when he starts earning some money.'

Alex took his father out into the sunshine. As they walked along they began to talk about the Reykjavik Chess Tournament between Boris Spassky and Bobby Fischer. Every day it was making the news. Spassky, the world champion and a Soviet citizen, had been suffering no end of ill manners and bizarre behaviour from Fischer, his American challenger. Frank had watched, appalled, when he had seen him on television.

'That man represents everything vain, egotistical and selfish about the West,' he spat.

'I agree,' said Alex. 'But the funny thing is, if Fischer hadn't been behaving so badly, then no one would care. Now even pop stations like Radio Luxembourg are relaying every move as it happens.'

It was true. Before the controversy, chess was played by serious boys and men with unfashionable haircuts. Now everyone was interested.

They walked past a hippie couple clad head to toe in denim. The boy was wearing a 'STOP THE WAR' badge and a T-shirt with a Peace sign in the colours of the American flag.

'Don't you think it's odd,' Frank said to Alex, 'how the West German youth claim to hate the Americans, especially over the Vietnam War, but they love their culture? Chewing gum, cowboy boots, blue jeans, rock music, Hollywood. They lap it up.'

Alex thought about that. 'America means money, glamour . . . all the things the Soviet Union never brought to our country,' he said. 'That's why we never felt like dressing up as Soviet peasants or playing a balalaika.'

Frank didn't reply, but he nodded. Alex was delighted. He had managed to say a couple of things his father had actually agreed with. After a second or two, he realised he was walking on his own. Frank had stopped to gawp in astonishment at a plumber's supply shop. There was a window display full of taps, sinks, shower fittings . . . You had to wait six months for stuff like that in the East. Here, you could go into a shop and buy it in sixty seconds.

Frank found a job quicker than they expected, in the telecommunications division of Siemens, the electronics giant. East German electrical engineers were valued. Their exemplary training and education more than made up for their unfamiliarity with the latest Western technology.

He was paid a generous salary – the rest of the family scoffed at how he had always said workers were exploited by the capitalists. Now he was working they were doing really well, especially as Gretchen had also found a job – teaching German in a local school. Their rent was reasonable. Soon they would be able to afford a BMW or a Mercedes.

But Frank was as bad-tempered as ever. In fact, he was more than that. He seemed sick in the soul. When they were alone one evening, Gretchen asked him quietly if he needed to see a doctor, even a psychiatrist, but he angrily rejected her suggestion.

CHAPTER 28

'Now we are settling in, we need to think about schools for the end of summer,' announced Gretchen one August morning. She took Alex and Geli to see several schools and colleges and they both found it strange walking into them and not being confronted with a picture of Honecker on every classroom wall.

Geli assembled an impressive portfolio of her best photographs. Within a week she had been offered a place at the Berlin State School of Fine Arts. The tutor who interviewed her said he had a friend who worked for the news magazine *Der Spiegel*. He was sure they would love to do a photo article about life in the East from a resident who had just escaped. Geli arrived home bursting with excitement but Frank was absolutely against the idea. 'We must not draw attention to ourselves.' Geli never sent the prints.

Alex was accepted at the local *Gymnasium*. He had to sit several exams and the rest of the family were surprised he'd got into such an academic school. 'You must have been paying some attention, after all,' said Frank. Alex was thrilled. It was unbelievable that he could be given a place in a school where his exam results, rather than his politics and appearance, would determine whether he went to university.

Frank Ostermann arrived on the first day of his job at Siemens feeling like the new boy at school who didn't know anybody. All his life he'd been told that capitalist businesses treated their workers with contempt and that backstabbing was the norm in the Western workplace.

So he was especially taken back when his department head – Herr Busch – greeted him with a handshake and told him that they were pleased to have someone of his calibre working on the team. He took him to meet the other department heads and made it plain that he should come to him at once if there were any problems.

'We know the value of experienced people. We know they can always get a job elsewhere.'

That was totally alien to Frank – touting your skills around and settling for the best offer. That was not what the 'socialist personality' did.

Busch told him he would find some of the Western technology more advanced, but he'd soon catch up. Too many of his workers, explained Busch, just expected things to work without really understanding them. Frank, he was sure, was a traditionalist. And he would be able to improvise when he needed to.

Frank noticed other differences. They didn't clock off at 1.00 on the dot for lunch – sometimes they even worked through their lunch hour. Sometimes they stayed late. It was a far cry from his job in East Berlin where the whole workshop downed tools as soon as the lunch whistle went and then all put on their coats the second the working day came to an end.

A week later his new colleagues all chipped in to buy him a birthday present and even bought him a cake. That evening, Busch and a couple of the others insisted Frank join them in Café Amsel, a nearby bar, for a couple of beers. The whole thing brought a lump to his throat.

On the way home, Frank stopped off to buy *Der Spiegel*. He noticed how everyone in the office made a habit of keeping up with the news and he did not want to feel left out.

That evening, Alex took *Der Spiegel* off to bed to read before he went to sleep. There was a major feature on the escapers from the East. It was a sorry catalogue of shootings and drownings. He didn't know whether to be pleased or disappointed that his family were not featured. Many of the escapers, Alex noted with a mixture of shock and admiration, had tried to swim across the River Spree at night, and in the middle of winter. Most of them had been shot in the water. There were also stories of young children falling in to the river on the Western side and drowning because only the East German border guards were allowed to enter the water. It seemed particularly cruel and senseless.

Then, as he turned to the final page of the piece, he

saw something which sent a chill down his spine. A familiar face stared back at him. The photo was captioned 'Holger Vogel, 16, shot dead whilst trying to escape, January 1972'. Alex read on with his heart in his mouth. Holger and an unknown girl had tried to cross over the Wall, said the article. They were spotted almost at once. She surrendered. He carried on running and they shot him. Poor Frau Vogel. He wondered if she was still waiting for the knock on the door to tell her he was all right. Alex had been certain he was dead, but seeing it there in black and white sickened his soul.

It had not been wise bedtime reading. Alex spent the night dreaming about his own escape and the rattle of machine guns that had accompanied it. He came to the breakfast table sunken-eyed and pale.

'Another bad night, *mein Schatz*?' said Gretchen, as she ruffled his hair.

Alex could bear it no longer. He had to find out if anyone else in the family had told anybody that they were going to escape.

'I have a confession to make,' he said. 'I told Sophie we were going.'

He heard his mother take a sharp intake of breath.

'I'm sorry,' he went on. 'I should have kept my mouth shut.'

There was an uncomfortable silence around the table.

Gretchen took his hand. 'Alex. She might have told the Stasi. That's probably why the lorry was stopped.'

'You stupid *Arschloch*, Alex. Do you know what you've done?' shouted Geli.

Alex dreaded his father's reaction the most. In fact, he had half expected Frank to get up and knock him off his chair. They all looked at him, waiting to see what he would do.

But Frank looked pained. He seemed neither angry nor surprised.

'It's my fault,' he said. 'If you want to be angry with anyone, blame me. I let you go out to see her. I should have told you ten minutes before we left. If I could have my time again, that is what I would do.'

Geli was steaming. 'Those two men, they might still be alive if he'd kept his mouth shut . . .'

Frank turned his anger on her. 'We have absolutely no proof whatsoever that Sophie betrayed us. Why would she? She was close to Alex . . . and even if she did tell, it was entirely the Stasi's decision to murder those two men. They could have arrested us and them easily enough. I think they did it to discourage other escape assistants.'

He thought for a while and then he said, 'And if they did know about the escape, why then did they not stop the lorry and search for us?'

Gretchen turned to Alex. 'And what do you think?' she asked.

Alex was fighting back his tears. 'I don't know, Mutti,' he said. 'The Stasi, they get to you. They even asked me if I would inform for them a couple of weeks before we escaped. I told them I'd think about it. I'm sure they would have been back to pester me, if we hadn't come here. They might even have threatened to arrest me again. Maybe they threatened Sophie to make her spy on me? Geli is right. I should have kept my mouth shut.'

Geli snorted with scorn. 'She should have kept her mouth shut too. The little snitch. No wonder she hasn't been round to Grandma's to ask how we were.'

'We shall never know if she reported us,' Gretchen said, 'and we shall never know if it was our fault those two men were murdered. But we must stop blaming ourselves. Vati is right. It was the Stasi who pulled the trigger on the machine guns, not us.'

CHAPTER 29

As the summer drew to a close the whole country was galvanised by the forthcoming spectacle of the Munich Olympics. The Ostermanns were all looking forward to watching it on television. The stadium, the pool, and the other new buildings around the site, looked like something out of a science fiction story. The whole event was a great showcase for West German architecture and technology.

And the East Germans – so all the Western newspapers reported – were determined to show the world how their 15 million people were going to produce superior athletes to the 55 million who lived in West Germany. What was it Honecker had said? The Deutsche Demokratische Republik was 'a victor of history' and would soon prove to be a victor on the athletics field too.

Alex could not get enough of the West German newspapers. There was a saying in the East: 'Twenty-three newspapers, four radio stations, two television channels, one opinion.' In the West you would have two articles in the same paper completely contradicting each other, or two different papers, both with opposing opinions. Alex loved the way he was allowed to make up his mind about what was going on, rather than being spoon-fed with an opinion he was not allowed to disagree with.

He read a paper every morning as he ate his breakfast. One particular story nearly made him choke on his rye bread.

'Hey, Geli,' he shouted. 'Come and have a look at this.'

She came in from the bathroom, towel drying her hair.

'Look. It says here that East German athletes are being given drugs to make them faster and stronger.'

Geli was a little cynical. 'That's just sour grapes, isn't it? They're making excuses in case the Western athletes don't do as well.'

But as they both read on something in the story began to ring horribly true. It said that the drugs were called steroids and they had drastic side effects. They made athletes aggressive, bad-tempered and, with girls, they affected how the body developed, especially if they were taken by teenagers. Even worse, claimed the articles, the East German coaches did not even tell their charges they were being given steroids. They told them they were 'vitamin supplements'.

They both looked at each other. 'We have to tell Lili!' said Geli. 'We have to get to Munich.'

That evening, over the family supper, they begged their parents to let them travel there.

'Vati, the last few times I saw her she was like a different person,' said Alex. 'So angry and always looking for a fight. And she looks so manly these days. I'm sure those pills are doing terrible things to her.'

'Sour grapes,' said Frank. 'It's because our system is so much better than theirs at training athletes.'

They always noticed how he still said 'Us' and 'Them' about the East and the West; 'Us' was definitely the East.

'Please let us go to Munich, Vati,' pleaded Alex. He felt like his nine-year-old self asking Frank for another ten minutes out in the park when it was bedtime. 'We can go to the Games and see if we can meet up with Lili there. Go and watch her swim, maybe talk to her at the poolside?'

Frank thought hard for a minute.

'Alex, you know she'll be surrounded by security people. What if the Stasi see you and recognise you as someone who has just escaped. What if they try to kidnap you?'

'Come on, Vati,' scoffed Alex. 'This isn't James Bond . . . Look, we really need to talk to her – tell her about these drugs she's taking. She thinks they're vitamins. I think they're doing her terrible harm.'

'Let them go, Frank,' said Gretchen softly, as she put her arms around his shoulders. He had been an awful strain to live with since they had arrived in the West. Perhaps being away from the children, just being with her in the apartment, even for a couple of days, would make him more relaxed.

Frank relented. 'You go with Geli. I'll give you the fare for a trip to Munich. You'll have to sleep on the train – I don't think we have the money to put you up in a hotel. Besides, the hotels in Munich will be full of tourists.'

On the day before Lili's race, Alex and Geli left Zoo Station in the early evening to catch a connection to Hannover. They were loaded down with bread, cheese and sausages, and two flasks of coffee. In the gathering dusk after their train had left West Berlin, they watched the East German countryside flash by as the train headed towards the West German border. Everything outside the carriage window was dull and flat and dirty. They passed scrappy towns and villages that were almost deserted.

Although they were excited to be heading towards West Germany, both felt uneasy and began to wonder if it was wise to have gone on this trip. If the train was stopped and the border guards came to check passes, what would prevent them arresting Alex and Geli as escapers? They had their new West German passports now, but would that be enough to protect them?

The train did not stop. And when they reached the West German border, everything changed. There was a full moon and in its silvery glow they could see the countryside looked better cared for. Bright lights burned in the well-maintained towns and villages. After changing trains at Hannover they slept as they thundered south.

Around the same time Alex and Geli's train left Berlin, Frank was leaving work. Every Thursday evening, on the way home from the Siemens office, he stopped off at a café in Turmstrasse. The meeting was short – barely more than a couple of words and a brisk exchange of envelopes. His contact was usually a shifty young man he knew as Ulrich, who took his offering without comment. This Thursday a familiar face was waiting for him. It was Erich Kohl, the agent who had questioned him at Normannenstrasse.

'We shall take a stroll, Herr Ostermann,' he instructed.

They walked from Turmstrasse to Birkenstrasse, the next U-Bahn stop along, and Kohl spoke to him quietly but firmly. 'We are growing weary of your lack of progress. The information you are sending us is of no use whatsoever. We need to see some cutting edge results.'

'Herr Kohl, I am doing everything I can. It is a closely monitored office and the latest technology is not something that is available to everyone.'

'Take them to the Café Amsel, buy them a beer, see if you can get their tongues to wag,' said Kohl. 'We are starting to lose patience. I will give you another month. Ulrich has gone. You now have me to answer to.'

The remark about the Café Amsel really shook Frank. Was someone trailing him or did they have another insider at the office? Maybe both? What frightened Frank the most was that if they were following him at work, perhaps they would try to follow him home too. He would have to be careful. He was beginning to realise, too late, that whatever was good about the East had been completely eclipsed by the sinister men who controlled it.

When Geli and Alex woke, it was light outside and the train was only an hour away from Munich. Over a breakfast roll and coffee they formulated a plan. Geli would buy a 'Good Luck' card and address it to Lili. They would put a note in telling her their address and telephone number so she could get in touch with them and also several newspaper cuttings they had brought with them, all about the dangers of taking steroids. Now, if they could not get to speak to Lili, they would just give her the envelope. It would be an innocent enough gesture – fans giving her a good luck card. She would recognise her friends and know to keep the card from them.

The Olympics had been billed as 'The Happy Games' and the authorities were making every effort to ensure there could be no comparison with the 1936 Berlin Olympics hosted by the Nazis. The city was bursting with colourfully dressed tourists and the excitement of the day was contagious. The contrast with the grey dour streets of East Berlin was overwhelming. Everywhere they looked, among the brash advertising, was the bright blue solar logo of the Games, and images of the Olympic mascot – Waldi the multicoloured dachshund.

'Isn't it great to see all these adverts and these Olympic signs, and not one picture of Karl Marx and Erich Honecker!' said Alex.

'And no square-jawed socialist supermen!' said Geli. They liked the look of Waldi. There was absolutely nothing about him that suggested the burning urgency of increasing the grain harvest or cement quota or the need to emancipate yourself from the false consciousness of bourgeois consumerism.

On the way to the stadium they bought a paper. The steroid story was in the news again. One of the East German women's swimming team coaches had been questioned about why his girls looked so masculine and why some of them had such deep voices. Was this because they were taking steroids?

He was evasive. 'My girls have come to Munich to swim, not sing,' he said.

When they got to the pool, there were hundreds of people milling around outside, and touts selling tickets at four times the asking price. The day's events were sold out.

'We couldn't afford it anyway,' said Geli. 'Maybe this was not our brightest idea.'

'Then let's look for the athletes' entrance,' said Alex. 'There's got to be one somewhere. We can pretend we're after an autograph.'

The pool complex was a magnificent edifice of glass and steel. They wandered all around it and eventually found the right entrance. Here, they waited all day, taking refuge from the bright sunlight in the shadows close to the walls. Inside, they could hear the PA announcing each event and the crowd cheering the races and their victors.

They were hungry, so Geli went to buy sausages and drinks from the street vendors who ringed the stadium. They could never get over how expensive these things were in West Berlin and Geli was even more outraged by the prices in Munich. She bought one sausage roll and a can of coke for them both to share.

'Capitalism,' she fumed when she got back to Alex. 'There should be a law against this. It is pure exploitation.'

Alex laughed. 'The days of the five-*Pfennig* roll are over. Not everything Vati hates about the West is unreasonable.'

They spent the afternoon listening to a variety of national anthems and even heard Lili's name announced before a race. They were disappointed to hear she was not among the medal winners.

Late in the afternoon the East German team came out of the athletes' entrance to board a minibus back to their accommodation at the Olympic Village. They spotted Lili at once in her blue Olympic tracksuit, there in the middle of them all, surrounded by security people.

The team were mobbed by autograph hunters and Alex knew this was the one chance he was going to get. He pushed past the burly coaches and security men, who he was certain were Stasi, and barged up to Lili. 'Good luck card for you,' he shouted, and gave her the envelope. He looked her in the eye to make sure she had seen it was him and winked. Before she could say anything, he vanished into the crowd.

Alex and Geli hurried to the station without looking back. Although they had scoffed at Frank, they had half expected the East German security men to come after them.

Alex felt elated. His plan had succeeded. A train for Hannover and Berlin was leaving in ten minutes. Their carriage was not crowded. After they had wolfed down the bread and sausages they bought at the station, and had drunk their bottles of beer, they managed to stretch out on the seats and sleep. Alex drifted off, feeling he had done a good deed. Perhaps in the grand scheme of his life he had redeemed himself for telling Sophie they were going and allowing her to betray them. Now Lili knew about her 'vitamin pills', she would surely refuse to continue taking them.

Back in Munich one of the Stasi officers delegated to watch the team and ensure there were no defectors used a paper knife to open the envelope Alex had taken so much trouble to deliver. He had removed it from Lili Weber's hands almost as soon as Alex had given it to her. She had been trouble all along, that one. And she was on a final warning. Any further insolence and lack of cooperation and she would be on a plane straight back to Berlin. A sealed envelope from a fan outside the stadium was exactly the sort of unofficial access the Stasi men were trained to prevent.

At first he thought the envelope might contain

instructions from outside accomplices on how to escape. Then Lili Weber would really be for it. Four or five years in a *Jugendwerkhof*.

But it didn't. Lili was off the hook. Still, the contents were very interesting. The officer read the newspaper cuttings, which he dismissed as capitalist disinformation, and took a careful note of the West Berlin contacts who had given it to her. The Stasi knew Lili Weber had never been out of the Eastern Bloc in her life, so these people would have to have been friends of hers from East Berlin. They must be border violators.

CHAPTER 30

Colonel Theissen received another memo from Kohl the next afternoon.

```
LATCH is now operational for Central
Reconnaissance Administration Science and
Technology Sector. Operative 122 in the
Western Sector successfully complied with
order to enable placement at Siemens
facility in West Berlin before
redeployment. LATCH's knowledge of
electronics makes him especially
suitable. (He has been compelled to sign
declaration of obligations prior to
insertion.) So far, information arriving
is of limited use. Further coercive
pressure may be necessary and I have now
taken on this responsibility.

Further consideration should also be
given to whether BOLT and LOCK could be
utilised as agents capable of infiltrating
```

```
and reporting on Federal Republic youth
groups. Previous asocial and negative-
decadent tendencies suggest coercive
means would be necessary to ensure
cooperation. Request permission to
proceed in this matter.
```

Kohl was really getting into his stride on this operation, thought Theissen. If all went well, there was the prospect of a promotion for both of them. He reached for another report just arrived on his desk and began drafting a response:

```
Request approved. Your successful
execution of this operation, so far, has
been noted.
Sektion XII has now obtained details of
LATCH domestic residence:
Bellermannstrasse 90
Wedding
Telephone
Wedding 885 53
As BOLT and LOCK and KEY are security to
ensure cooperation of LATCH in
infiltration of Siemens, suggest immediate
non-violent conspirative opening for
placement of listening devices.
```

CHAPTER 31

Alex started his new school just as the Munich Games took a nightmare turn. Palestinian gunmen, calling themselves the Black September Organisation, broke into the Olympic village and took Israeli athletes hostage. The talk in the school canteen was of nothing else. When the siege ended in a massacre, the country was shocked and sickened. They all watched the terrible news footage of the hushed stadium and the burned-out helicopters.

Alex had some sympathy with the Palestinians. The East German government always portrayed them as victims of the Israelis. He tried to talk to his fellow students about it, but it made him unpopular.

Alex didn't help himself. One lunchbreak he joined some classmates who were playing Monopoly. They explained it to him in condescending tones. 'So you have to buy up as much property as possible and then fleece all the other players for rent?' he exclaimed. Alex thought the game should be called 'Grasping capitalist landlord'. It seemed bizarre to celebrate this particularly ugly aspect of Western life in a board game. He told Geli about it that evening. 'They'll be inventing a game where you pretend to be a drug dealer or a pimp next,' she said. 'It's revelling in the worst human instincts.'

Alex's classmates seemed to think he was too gauche, too enthusiastic about things. He wasn't 'cool'. In the East he had been the class rebel. Now he was that awkward kid in the ill-fitting jeans, from the other side of the Wall.

But even if he didn't feel comfortable with his peers, Alex enjoyed his lessons and time in the school library. He hoovered up new knowledge at every opportunity. He especially liked history, now it wasn't taught as an exercise in Marxist-Leninist propaganda.

Music had always been Alex's great love, and it did not let him down. A few weeks into term he found himself alone, as usual, in a school lunchbreak. At these awkward times he had taken to visiting the school music rooms. Here he would pick up a guitar or tootle around on a piano. That lunchtime a couple of lads wandered over to listen and made some appreciative noises about his guitar playing. One of them asked, 'Can you do "Starman"?'

Alex had seen David Bowie playing it on West German TV that summer, and he sketched out an approximation of the song. Bowie's appearance, with his band The Spiders from Mars, had provoked equal parts outrage and admiration. Frank had almost choked on his beer when he saw the make-up and the costumes and the platform boots, and swore horribly. That made Alex like Bowie even more.

The other lad showed Alex the two strange chords that started the song. That was nice, he thought. Learning something new. As they chatted away, they agreed that Bowie and his band may look weird, but they really liked their music. Geli had got hold of a copy of 'Ziggy Stardust'. Alex thought it was a pretty daft title, but he loved the songs – especially the one called 'Moonage Daydream', which had a guitar solo at the end that seemed to somersault off into space.

The boys introduced themselves as Andreas and Kurt. They told Alex about all the other bands they had seen at the Deutschlandhalle – Pink Floyd, The Who, Jimi Hendrix a few years back, and Led Zeppelin.

'They came two years ago,' said Kurt. '*Mein Gott*, it was loud. I'm surprised you didn't hear it on the other side of the Wall.'

Alex should go with them, they said, when the next good band came along.

Then Andreas said he and Kurt played in a group and they had room for another guitar player. When Alex told them he had left his gear behind in the East, they said he could borrow some of theirs, and he should come over to their rehearsal space at the weekend.

Alex walked back to Bellermannstrasse full of hope. Maybe he wouldn't feel so much of an outsider if he was in a band. Gretchen was delighted to see him come home with a spring in his step. He had been so glum returning from school in the first few weeks. She wished she could see Frank walk in through the front door with a smile on his face. Hadn't he said his work was interesting and

216

everyone treated him very well? She couldn't understand why he was so unhappy.

At that moment Frank was walking between U-Bahn stops and talking to Herr Kohl. They were very disappointed with the quality of intelligence he was providing from Siemens. This time Kohl's threats were more explicit.

'I have several colleagues who would like to see your son and daughter extracted. In their absence they have been sentenced to lengthy prison terms for their desertion of the DDR. We can pick them up easily enough and have them back in the East in less than an hour. If they cause any trouble, I don't like to think what will happen to them.'

Frank stopped dead in his tracks. 'If you do anything to my children, I shall strangle you with my bare hands,' he said, trying to keep his voice down. But Kohl had already disappeared into the milling crowd of early evening commuters.

When Kohl returned to Normannenstrasse, he drafted a memo to Theissen seeking authorisation from the highest level to have Alex and Geli returned to East Berlin. It might not be necessary, but Frank Ostermann was proving to be less cooperative than they had hoped. It was good practice to be prepared for the next stage of coercive action.

CHAPTER 32

Now he felt more settled at school, being in West Berlin filled Alex with an energy he didn't know he had. It was like having an extra battery in your system. He managed to hold down his jobs and still get his school work done. He enjoyed being able to ask whatever questions he liked in school, without wondering whether he would be criticised for 'false opinions'.

Geli had started college in early October. The other students looked on her like a poor relation. There was always an uncomfortable silence when she joined her year group in the college canteen. Then one of them would ask whether they had fruit or television over in the East.

She shrugged it off and told her family it would pass.

It did. By the time autumn was turning to winter, the telephone in the Ostermann apartment was always ringing. Frank and Gretchen never answered it. It was always for one of their kids. This was one of the luxuries of the West that Geli and Alex really enjoyed. In the East only government people, doctors and a few other professionals had phones in the home. Here, everyone had one.

Frank flinched every time it rang. He had wanted to

have it disconnected but the children made such a fuss he relented. Frank knew that a telephone was another way for the Stasi to get to him. So far they had not called, and he was beginning to hope this was because they did not know either of his contact numbers.

But when his office phone went and it was Kohl, that hope was extinguished. 'Hello, Frank, it's Volker,' said the voice he recognised at once. Kohl sounded very friendly – a ruse no doubt to make the conversation seem as innocent as possible, in case anyone else was listening in. 'I can't meet you for lunch, so how about we have a quick drink in Pankstrasse tomorrow – there's a bar right by the U-Bahn. The Sapphire. Six thirty. See you there.'

The line went dead before Frank could reply.

He didn't like the idea of meeting with Kohl so close to his own home. It would make it easier for Kohl to follow him. Or one of the family might see him. And Grandma Ostermann was coming tomorrow. Gretchen was cooking her an early evening supper.

He would just have to hope the meeting was a short one. There was still little to report. So far, nothing had come across Frank's desk that would be of great interest to the Stasi. Surely Kohl could not be serious with his threats? Surely they knew things like this took time – months or years?

Frank spent an anxious day at work, finding it difficult to settle on anything. At the end of the day when he walked into the Sapphire, Kohl was already sitting there

219

waiting for him. The meeting was brief. Kohl said, 'We are not happy with your behaviour. We know there is more that you can do to help us. But to show our good will I have something here that will help you.'

He put his hand into the inside pocket of his jacket to pull out an envelope when a startled expression flickered across his face and he stopped. Kohl was looking at one of the men in the bar. He discreetly slipped the envelope back inside his jacket.

'I have to go,' he said. 'Follow me in two minutes. Meet me in the ticket hall in the U-Bahn.'

Kohl slipped out of the door.

Frank waited in the bar, wondering what it was that had made Kohl leave in such a hurry. After a couple of minutes he left the bar and went down the steps to the underground as Kohl had instructed. He found him lurking near a shop kiosk with his back to the milling crowd of U-Bahn passengers. Frank had never seen Kohl like this. He definitely seemed ruffled.

'Here take this.' Kohl handed over the envelope. Then he grabbed Frank's arm and squeezed it painfully. 'You will read it when you are alone and then destroy the contents. And don't forget what I said about Alex and Geli. We know where you live and we know exactly where to find them.' Then he was gone.

Frank hurried home to the apartment and put the envelope beside his bed. Thirty seconds later the doorbell chimed. It was Grandma Ostermann.

'What a chilly night,' she announced to no one in particular. Then she turned to her son.

'Frank, you do keep interesting company,' she said. Frank blushed hot and cold.

'What are you talking about?'

'That fellow who I saw you with at the station. The one who grabbed your arm and looked like a policeman. Who is he? You looked frightened to death.'

Gretchen was all ears. 'Which fellow? What's the matter, Frank? You look as white as a sheet.'

Frank was reeling. He knew with terrible clarity that the Stasi would stop at nothing to get what they wanted. They were never going to leave him alone and the noose was closing around them all. Something snapped in him. He decided it was time to tell them everything.

'Let's sit down and have a drink. Is Geli in? Where is Alex?' he said quietly.

'Geli's in her room. Alex telephoned to say he's gone to the Deutschlandhalle with Andreas and Kurt,' said Gretchen. 'The Rolling Stones are coming. They are queuing to buy tickets.'

'Call Geli in. I have something to tell you.'

When Geli came in, they all looked at Frank, waiting to hear what he had to say.

He switched on the radio and turned the volume up as loud as it would go. He had always hoped the Stasi did not know where they lived but now he realised that had been naive – even stupid.

'Frank, what on earth are you doing?' said Gretchen.

Frank put a finger to his lips and pointed to the table. He picked up a notepad and biro and wrote 'BUG'.

'But they can't do that here, not in the West, surely?' Gretchen said loudly.

Frank was getting agitated and gestured for her to keep her voice down.

'We can't be sure,' he whispered. 'Now come closer and listen to me.'

Gretchen was wide-eyed with astonishment. She could barely contain her exasperation at having to conduct a conversation like this in hoarse whispers. 'So, the only reason we're here is because you agreed to spy for the Stasi?'

Frank was getting angry. 'What else could I do? They threatened to send Alex and Geli to prison. What would you have done, Gretchen?'

'I would have told you about it,' she said. There were tears in her eyes.

'I didn't want to burden you with it. Besides, I was made to sign a statement of obligation where I swore I would not speak to anyone about it.'

'I am not just *anyone*, Frank . . .' said Gretchen.

Frank realised at that moment how forty years of living in East Berlin had affected him. How he had considered the State, and its authority, more important than his own wife. How he had not even dared to tell her what sort of mess he had got himself into.

'I thought I would agree and get us all out. Then when

we were over here I would try and extract myself from this awful situation. I knew they were going to get me into Siemens.'

'We have to go,' said Geli. 'Get away from this Kohl fellow. Go to Munich or Bonn, somewhere where they can't get to us so easily. Vati, you have to go to the police, tell them everything.'

'Look, if it was that simple, I would have done it as soon as we arrived. They told me, when I came over, they would track me down if I tried to get away. They have spies all over the country. They have spies in the police and the government.'

'Do you think it's true?' said Gretchen.

'They even said they would get me if I moved away from Germany. "Read the papers while you're over there," they said. "See how many exiles from the East – in London, in New York – meet a sticky end."'

Frank buried his head in his hands.

'Look at that huge office they have at Normannenstrasse. You don't think that's just for traffic offences and keeping an eye on a few longhairs, do you? And they said if I don't cooperate they will seize Geli and Alex and take them back. I can't risk that happening . . .'

Erich Kohl had asked Frank to meet him near his home for a reason. There was a listening post in an attic apartment close to the Ostermanns where he joined another Stasi operative, based permanently in the West. The Ostermanns' apartment had been easy enough to break into. Bugs had been placed all around the apartment with a radio transmitter to relay any conversation to the listening post. It was technology in its infancy and it only worked in close proximity to the transmitter. What they really needed was something that would work well at longer range. That was exactly the sort of information his Stasi minders hoped Frank Ostermann would supply from Siemens.

Kohl had instructed the operatives who manned the listening post to make sure they always recorded the Ostermanns after his weekly meetings with Frank. If Frank was going to betray them, those were the times when he would most likely talk to his wife or children. A voice-activated reel-to-reel tape recorder had been set up to capture their conversations.

Kohl could not hear much of the conversation that evening, but the distorted music from a blaring radio told him everything he needed to know. Frank had talked.

'What will you do?' said the man.

'I will show them I mean business,' said Kohl. 'I shall take the boy.'

CHAPTER 33

As Kohl hurried back to Pankstrasse U-Bahn, Franz Hübner was walking through the same chilly Berlin evening towards his brother-in-law's residence in Wilmersdorf. Hübner was the man Erich Kohl had seen in the bar. His presence there was not a coincidence. He had been disappointed to notice Kohl get up and leave and was fairly certain he was the reason for his sudden departure. Hübner had supposed that the black patch he wore over his right eye would have afforded some sort of disguise to someone who had not seen him for several years, but evidently he was still entirely recognisable.

Hübner had been following Kohl, on and off, for most of the year. The West German secret service – the BfV – knew all about Frank Ostermann and his placement at Siemens. Now they were just biding their time, waiting to pounce at the most expedient moment.

Hübner had a personal interest in Kohl, or Gunter Schneider as he also knew him. He had been working undercover on the other side four years ago. Kohl had arrested him. The interrogation had been robust. They had let him go soon afterwards in a spy swap at Checkpoint

Charlie. Thereafter, Hübner made it his mission in life to bring down the Stasi man who had beaten him so badly he had lost several teeth and the sight in his right eye.

A few weeks after they had released him back to the West, Hübner, recuperating at home, had been reading an illustrated English book about the Gestapo. There was a spread of photographs, mugshots from identification papers captured by the Allies at the end of the war, showing the faces of assorted Gestapo men. One of them, with 'DECEASED' stamped over it, looked familiar.

Further research at the archives of the recently established *Gedenkstätte Deutscher Widerstand* – Memorial for German Resistance – in Stauffenbergstrasse, confirmed that this was Gunter Schneider. When Hübner found out, he punched the air. But when he talked to his commanding officer, he was completely uninterested. Hübner was sent out of his office with a flea in his ear. He began to wonder if his boss was working for the other side, or whether he was an old Gestapo man himself. He was certainly the right age – what the radical students called 'the Auschwitz Generation'.

So Hübner bided his time. Over the next couple of years, during the course of his work, he had picked up whatever useful information he could. They had sources in the Stasi's Normannenstrasse headquarters who provided them with intelligence. Hübner knew, for example, that Kohl's superior was a Colonel Theissen. He also knew that Theissen had a deep and abiding hatred for the Nazis. As a Communist 'agitator', he had survived six years in Dachau concentration camp. Hübner thought anyone who could do that must have iron for blood. He felt some affinity with Theissen and thought it a shame that they were on opposite sides. Hübner's own father had named him Franz after the uncle he had never known who was executed by the Gestapo for distributing leaflets calling for an end to the war.

Now was the time, judged Hübner, to let the Stasi know who Erich Kohl actually was. If Hübner's commanding officer was not interested, then he would send the information directly to Colonel Theissen himself. Hübner photocopied the Gestapo mugshot from the book. He typed 'Erich Kohl is Gunter Schneider' on a piece of paper, just to make it crystal clear, attached it to the copy of the photo with a paperclip and placed both in an envelope. His brother-in-law was visiting an uncle in East Berlin tomorrow. He would ask him to post it there.

He smiled at the simplicity of his plan. This was far more efficient than arresting Kohl or having him killed. Such an action usually provoked bloody retaliation. Besides, an arrest would just lead to a tit for tat swap somewhere down the line. Let them deal with their own *Schund und Schmutz*. Whatever fate the Stasi would mete out to Erich Kohl would be far more interesting than anything the West German secret service could do to him.

CHAPTER 34

The Ostermanns sat round their dining table and tried to eat. The neighbours had complained about the radio so now they sat there in a strained silence. No one could think of anything to say.

Frank did try to convince his mother that she would be safer if she stayed in West Berlin. He scribbled his thoughts on the notepad. Grandma Ostermann could not be persuaded.

'What would the Stasi want with me?' she wrote.

Alex had still not returned by the time she left to catch a tram from Sonnenallee back to Treptower Park. After Gretchen came back from taking her to the U-Bahn station, they had another desperate, whispered conversation, with the radio on more quietly this time.

'The police, you must go to them, Vati, or the secret service,' Geli said.

Frank was beside himself with anxiety. It didn't make coming to a logical conclusion any easier. 'How the hell am I supposed to contact the secret service?' he hissed.

None of them had the first idea, but they thought if they went to the police they would know.

Frank calmed down and they worked out a plan. When Alex got back, all four of them would go down to the police station on Prinzenallee. Frank would tell them everything and ask for the whole family to be taken into police protection. They would just have to hope the Stasi were bluffing about their spies in government and trust they were dealing with honest people.

Kohl knew he had to get to Alex Ostermann immediately. For all the threats he had made to Frank, having the Ostermann children sent back to East Berlin would take too long to arrange. Mere hours remained to save the situation. It was true that they had spies in the police and the highest level of government. But their coverage was patchy and could not be relied on.

Kohl knew Alex would be home soon so he waited for him at Pankstrasse U-Bahn. Gretchen and Grandma Ostermann walked straight past him as they hurried down to the underground at 9.00 that evening. Kohl wondered whether to seize Gretchen instead. He decided she would be too much trouble.

It was past 10.00 when Alex came up the stairs with his prized Rolling Stones concert tickets – one for him and one for Geli. His friends had both bought four tickets – intending to sell their spare ones for double or more their value. 'It's bound to sell out, so let's make a bit of money out of it!' said Andreas. Alex couldn't bring himself to do that. Why deprive someone else further back in the queue of the chance to buy a ticket just so you could make a bit of extra money? It was seedy.

Lost in thought, he didn't see Kohl until he had grabbed his arm and dragged Alex into one of the shop doorways in the U-Bahn underpass.

'Alex Ostermann,' said Kohl, 'come with me if you want to live.'

Alex flinched as he recognised him. He tried to break away but Kohl had an iron grip. What else could he do? A couple of young men who had followed Alex off the train walked past. Alex cried out for help. They looked alarmed and uncertain.

'Police,' said Kohl with brisk confidence. 'Move along.'

They were easily persuaded. Kohl certainly didn't look like a mugger.

'Have you got that?' said Kohl with venom in his voice. 'I look like a policeman. You look like trouble.'

As they waited for a southbound train, Alex kept looking up and down the empty platform, hoping someone would arrive who would help him. Maybe Frank would come down with Grandma? Then he'd be all right. Kohl knew exactly what he was doing and whispered, 'I have an accomplice tailing us. If you run off, he has instructions to kill you. Either him or me can snuff you out in an instant, so do exactly as I tell you.'

Alex didn't know whether to believe him. Was this man lurking on the concourse above the platforms? He hadn't noticed anyone else up there. He heard the distant rumble of a train and hoped it would be one coming up from the centre and some of the passengers getting off would be friends from school. His instinct told him that the further he got away from home, the more difficult it would be to escape.

A southbound train burst from the tunnel and Alex felt his hopes drain away. Kohl dragged him into a carriage just as a young man ran down the stairs and boarded the train. Alex wondered if Kohl really did have an accomplice. But there was no eye contact, no recognition, between Kohl and the other man.

Kohl hissed, 'Keep your mouth shut. No one is going to help you.'

Alex thought he could try to break away when they changed trains, especially after he noticed Kohl's 'accomplice' stayed on the train when they got off at Gesundbrunnen. Kohl realised this too, and held on to his arm particularly tightly as they hurried through the empty white-tiled tunnels.

The only way he was going to get out of this, thought Alex, was by spotting a real policeman and asking him to call Kohl's bluff. But his luck had deserted him that night.

Their journey came to an end at Görlitzer Bahnhof in Kreuzberg. They walked for ten minutes through dark empty streets until they came to a cheap and anonymous apartment block. Kohl had a sparsely furnished studio room four floors up, in a turn-of-the-century block.

As soon as they got there, Kohl tied Alex to a chair at gunpoint.

'Keep your trap shut,' he said. Then he picked up the phone and dialled a number.

'Hello, Frank,' he said. 'Volker here. Alex would like to talk to you.'

Kohl held a knife to Alex's throat with one hand and the telephone next to his mouth with the other. 'Just say hello,' he said calmly.

'Vati,' said Alex.

'Are you all right?' said Frank

Kohl spoke into the phone. 'Have you had time to read my letter?' he said, then he put the phone down.

Alex watched with mounting dread and wondered what on earth was going to happen next. Kohl walked into the kitchenette off the main studio room. Alex heard a drawer opening, then rattling, then tearing noises. Kohl returned with a strip of black insulating tape which he placed roughly over Alex's mouth. Then he ruffled his hair, like a hearty *Onkel*.

'You just sit tight and be a good boy,' he said.

Gretchen and Geli sat in shocked silence. They were all stunned. Eventually Gretchen whispered, 'Do you think Kohl knew we intended to go to the police?'

'I don't know, but something made them take Alex,' Frank replied.

Geli wrote 'We have definitely been bugged' on the kitchen notepad.

They spent the next hour combing the apartment

looking for listening devices. Frank found something odd in the telephone but decided not to remove it in case it broke the phone. It could just as easily be a piece of West German technology he did not recognise. They couldn't find anything else.

Frank could put off opening Kohl's letter no longer. His hands were shaking so much he had to put it on the table in order to read it. The instructions were blunt.

Memorise then burn. Floor 6. Room 632. Combination 25894927. Fibre optics dossier.

'What do they mean, "Combination"?' said Gretchen.

Frank hushed her with a despairing motion and beckoned for them to step outside. They huddled together on the window ledge leading down to the apartment lobby.

'He's referring to a safe at Siemens,' said Frank, trying to pull himself together.

The Stasi had mentioned in their original briefing, before the escape, that they were interested in fibre optics technology – the transmission of light signals along minuscule glass tubes. It was at the cutting edge of communications technology. Frank and his colleagues back in East Berlin were familiar with the concept, but no one in the East was able to make glass tubes of sufficiently small dimension and quality to allow data to be transmitted without corrupting it.

'But how do they know the dossier is there?' whispered Gretchen. 'And how do they know the combination?

They must have someone else there working for them. So why doesn't he do it?'

Geli put a hand on her father's shoulder. 'They must think you're expendable . . . or maybe it's some sort of test?'

'Either way, I think I'm just going to have to do this,' Frank said. 'Stay in the apartment. While I'm out, don't answer the door to anyone.'

Frank supposed he would have to stay after work and wait for the cleaners to go home. Surely it couldn't be that simple?

But it was. He spent an agonising day at work trying to pretend everything was OK. It so plainly wasn't he ended up telling his colleagues his son was very ill. That bought him some sympathy but only brought him more attention. He spent the rest of the day fending off suggestions he should go home early to see his son. He told them he would rather keep his mind busy with his work than fret about it at home. His wife would ring if his son took a turn for the worse.

Eventually the working day came to an end. One by one, his colleagues left their desks. By seven o'clock, when they had all gone, Frank ventured up to the sixth floor. He knew Herr Busch worked up here – he could claim to be looking for his office if anyone challenged him.

There was no one around apart from an elderly Turkish woman, cleaning the offices at the far end of the corridor. Frank told himself if he looked like he knew exactly what he was doing then no one would think he was acting suspiciously.

He followed Kohl's instruction to the letter. The combination worked first time, and the safe swung open with a satisfying click. He didn't even steal the dossier. He just photocopied it on the Xerox machine at the end of the corridor. That was another piece of Western technology he couldn't quite believe. Every office had one. They were illegal in the DDR. The regime was afraid that dissidents would mass produce subversive leaflets. Only the most trusted government organisations had them.

When he had finished, he put the dossier back in the safe and locked it. Now they wouldn't even know he'd been to have a look. He didn't notice the security camera in the top right-hand corner of the corridor.

Geli and Gretchen were waiting anxiously at home, hoping for some news, when Frank got home that night. He asked if Kohl had rung the apartment. He hadn't. They waited until midnight willing Kohl to call and went to bed disappointed and exhausted.

The next day Frank felt so edgy at work he spilt his coffee when the lady came round with drinks and biscuits at 10.30. His phone went just after 11.00 and he nearly jumped out of his skin. It was the pensions department calling to discuss his monthly contribution. After he put the phone down he had to go to the lavatory to be sick.

He kept thinking about that dossier, sitting there at home underneath his bed. How long would they send him to prison for? Five, ten years? Industrial espionage was a most serious offence – particularly in this Cold War world. Frank could imagine the judge at his court case. 'We gave you, a refugee, a most generous welcome, and you have repaid us with this appalling betrayal . . .'

The phone went again at 5.10, just as he was getting ready to leave. '*Guten Abend*, Frank,' said the cheery voice. 'It's Volker here. Birthday party tonight. But you can only come if you have bought me a present.'

'I have,' said Frank, trying to sound equally cheerful and not quite making it. 'I have a very nice present for you.'

'Well then, you can meet me at the Café Olympia by Görlitzer Bahnhof. I'll be there at 8.00.'

'Will my friend Alex be there?' asked Frank, but when he got to the end of his sentence he could only hear the dialling tone.

Frank Ostermann set out that evening determined to see this whole thing through. He took his photocopied dossier and tucked it into his trouser waist. Lost in thought as he hurried down Bellermannstrasse and Prinzenallee to the U-Bahn, he barely noticed the freezing sleet and winter wind that pulled at his coat.

He expected the U-Bahn trip to Görlitzer Bahnhof to take at least half an hour. It was an awkward journey and he had to change three times. But Frank Ostermann had not expected to be arrested as he changed trains at Hallesches Tor.

'BfV,' said a man in a pale overcoat, as he hustled him to the side of the platform. He had a black patch over his right eye. Another man appeared in a similar overcoat and stood in front of him. 'Where are you going, sir?'

The platform was deserted now. Frank found their mock courtesy unsettling. 'I have to meet a friend at eight. Why have you stopped me?'

'Are you carrying any documents, sir?' said one of the men. They frisked him without waiting for an answer, took the folder from within his coat and briskly scanned through it.

'Frank Ostermann,' said the man who had originally seized him, 'I am arresting you on a charge of industrial espionage.'

Frank felt sick with fear. 'I have to meet this man, Erich Kohl,' he pleaded. 'He has my son as a hostage.'

'Erich Kohl,' said the man with the eyepatch. 'And where are you meeting him?'

Frank decided he had to tell them.

The men nodded to each other, and the one with the eyepatch handed the dossier back to Frank.

'You will carry on,' he said plainly. 'You need to keep your appointment.'

'What about my son?' said Frank, fighting the choking panic rising in his chest.

'Come,' said the other man, ignoring his question.

They took the next U-Bahn to Görlitzer Bahnhof, and when they came out into the street the other agent said, 'We will be following you within pistol range. Do not disappoint us, Frank Ostermann. It would be very easy for you to be shot whilst trying to escape.'

Frank found the Café Olympia quickly enough. Kohl was not there. Frank was ten minutes late. Maybe that had spooked him and he had gone.

Frank bought a beer and waited. The man without the patch came into the bar and sat on the other side. After another ten minutes the phone behind the counter rang.

'Do we have a Frank Ostermann in the bar?' asked the bartender.

Frank leapt to his feet.

The voice in the earpiece was instantly familiar. 'Ah, hello, Frank. I got tired of waiting so I went back home. Now there's no funny business is there, because if there is then Alex here will be meeting a sticky end. Say hello, Alex.'

Frank could hear muffled noises. Alex obviously had something over his mouth. He sounded very frightened.

'You will meet me outside, on the steps of the church,' said Kohl. The line went dead.

CHAPTER 35

The great red-brick church – Emmauskirche – was impossible to miss. Frank was standing on the steps less than two minutes later. The sleet had turned to driving rain. By the time Kohl came and stood next to him, Frank's hair was dripping.

'You were late,' said Kohl.

'What have you done with my son?' said Frank, trying to control his anger.

'He is fine. Alex is being a good boy. He has been no trouble. Perhaps he is a little hungry, and thirsty.'

Kohl had decided to take Frank back to the apartment to inspect the documents. Then he would kill him and Alex. His pistol was sitting there in his overcoat, silencer already attached. They would find the bodies eventually, when the smell alerted the other residents. Kohl would be long gone. It would be a shame to lose the apartment but he had already used it several times more than the manual said was prudent.

Frank lied. 'My train got stuck between stations.'

'*Natürlich*,' said Kohl. He didn't believe him but he didn't want to waste any more time out here. He felt too exposed.

Frank wondered where the BfV men were. They had promised to follow him from a distance. It was such a filthy night now, it would be difficult to make out who was who from more than a few metres, especially in these dark streets.

'You will come back to my apartment and show me the dossier,' said Kohl.

Frank was immediately suspicious. 'No. Let us go to another bar.' Why would Kohl want to take him to somewhere private unless he intended to kill him?

Kohl was placatory. 'You want to see your son, don't you? Alex is there. I want to look at those plans, Frank. In a good light, away from prying eyes. Then Alex will be free to go. Come. I need ten more minutes of your life. If you have got our documents, as we instructed, then you will have fulfilled your obligation to us.'

He hoped those BfV men were close behind.

'Come,' said Kohl.

The chair Alex Ostermann had been tied to was placed in the centre of the studio apartment, facing into the room. There was one large window, curtains permanently drawn, overlooking an internal courtyard. Alex had measured the days by watching the light fade and then return but he had lost track of exactly how long he had been there.

The insulating tape placed over his mouth was itching terribly and he felt utterly terrified. At first, it was a stark, blind kind of terror, the sort that had made him wriggle to try to get free, when Kohl was away from the apartment, and cut his wrists on the ropes that held him. When Kohl came to check the ropes and noticed, that had earned him a painful box around the ears.

Now Alex's fear had settled into a dull sensation, like a toothache, but in the pit of his stomach. Kohl had given him very little to eat and drink since he'd taken him to the apartment. He was hungry and very thirsty and had a horrible sour taste in his mouth. He was light-headed too from lack of sleep, and felt like he was drifting in and out of a drowsy nightmare.

Kohl had been gone more often than he was there, and when he was away Alex had tried to make as much noise as possible with a black insulating strip over his mouth. The woman upstairs had heard his grunts and squeals and had banged heavily on the floor and shouted 'Um Gottes Willen, du bist pervers!' – 'For heaven's sake, you're sick!' This had happened a couple of times. Alex was so thirsty now he had difficulty making any noise at all.

Kohl had gone to get Frank and what would happen next was anyone's guess. Would he shoot them both or would he let them go? Alex felt utterly helpless – he would just have to see.

He heard the door open and shut and looked up expecting to see Kohl and his Vater. To his amazement he found himself staring at a young man carrying a small pistol. He was wearing an army surplus combat jacket, orange loon pants, and had shoulder-length brown hair and the sort of scrubby beard students grow. He and Alex were equally astonished to see each other.

In a flash the man came over and ripped away the tape from Alex's mouth, leaving it dangling at the side of his cheek. His mouth burned with the pain and Alex cried out. His lips were cracked and peeling from having so little to drink and now they were bleeding profusely.

'Who the hell are you?' said the man.

Alex croaked out his name. He could barely speak.

'Water,' he managed to say.

The man went over to the kitchenette at the side of the room and swiftly filled a glass from the draining board. He held it to Alex's lips and let him take several gulps then put it down on a sideboard.

'I've been kidnapped by this Stasi man,' said Alex.

'Do you know his name?'

'Erich Kohl.'

'Good,' said the man.

'Are you police?' said Alex, who was bewildered by his response.

'Yeah,' said the man in a sarcastic tone.

Alex was beginning to feel frightened all over again. 'Please help get me out.'

There was a scuffle at the door. The man quickly placed the tape back over Alex's mouth.

He heard a ruffling noise behind him and guessed the fellow must be hiding on the step behind the curtain.

Kohl came in with Frank, who immediately rushed to Alex's side.

Kohl drew his pistol and barked, 'Stay away from him. Sit down over there and give me the dossier.' The placatory tone had vanished.

Frank spotted the silencer and his worst fears were confirmed. He was sure Kohl was going to kill them both at any second. He wondered whether to rush Kohl while he handed over the dossier.

But just as Kohl snatched away the file, his eyes alighted on a half empty glass of water on the sideboard. The side of the glass was smeared with blood . . .

Frank noticed too and decided this was his moment, but Kohl was an old hand and knew exactly what Frank was thinking.

He waved the gun at Frank, gesturing for him to get down on the floor. Frank knelt down. Kohl tossed the dossier on to the table then angrily waved his gun some more, indicating Frank should lie face down.

Alex looked on in helpless horror. *This is it*, he thought. A cold-blooded execution. First Vater, then me. He could not bear to look and screwed up his eyes.

Frank stared at the wooden floorboards, thinking this was the last thing he would ever see. His heart was thumping so hard. Where the hell were those two West German policemen? They should have been right behind him. Out of the corner of his eye he could see Kohl had moved to the side of the room. What on earth was he doing?

243

Kohl switched off the light. In the darkness the intruder was backlit by the street light in the courtyard below and appeared as a silhouette against the curtain.

Now everything happened at once. Kohl drew a bead on the figure and squeezed the trigger of his pistol. Just as he fired his target darted swiftly from his hiding place. The window shattered and glass skittered down to the courtyard below. The woman in the apartment above cried out in alarm. The intruder began to shoot blindly in Kohl's direction. With plaster and wood splintering and disintegrating around him, Frank hurriedly crawled to Alex and pushed his son's chair over, out of the line of fire.

Disorientated by the noise of the shots, and the now piercing screams of the woman upstairs, Kohl's survival instinct told him to flee. He slammed the door, ran out of the flat and leaped down the stairs, taking them three at a time. On the first-floor landing he ploughed straight into Franz Hübner and his colleague with such force he knocked both of them over. As they staggered to their feet a second figure ran past and out into the street. They were so stunned they noticed little more than a flash of orange trousers.

Shots rang out in the street. Hübner and his colleague hurried out to find a crumpled figure in the rain-drenched gutter. It was a young man with the bright orange trousers. He was bleeding profusely from his abdomen. The man tried to stand up and stagger away, but he collapsed again immediately.

With Kohl and the intruder gone, Frank found the light switch and hurried over to Alex. He lifted him and the chair up gently and gingerly removed the gag from his mouth.

'I thought he was going to shoot you,' Alex said, as his father untied him. 'And who was that other man?' He felt sick and his hands were shaking. He didn't know if he would be able to stand up unaided.

They had both heard the commotion on the stairs and the shots in the street and by now the landing outside the open door to the apartment had filled with frightened residents. One of the crowd, a woman in her thirties, was hysterical – perhaps she was the upstairs neighbour.

They were safe now there were people around. Frank went to the door and called for someone, anyone, to call the police.

'They're here already,' said a gruff older man.

Hübner had rushed back up the stairs two at a time. He looked relieved when he saw Frank. 'What's happening?' he asked breathlessly. 'Is your son there? Is he all right?'

'No thanks to you,' said Frank. 'What the hell kept you?'

Hübner held his hands open. 'I'm sorry. We had to make sure he didn't spot us. That would have been fatal for you both.'

He walked into the apartment and put an arm on Alex's shoulder. 'Can you walk or do you need a stretcher?' he asked.

Alex croaked, 'I need water.' His arm felt as though it might have fractured where he had landed on it when Frank knocked his chair over, but now he was free he could feel his strength returning.

'When you're ready, take him downstairs to wait for an ambulance,' Hübner said to Frank.

Alex stumbled downstairs, past the bewildered stares of the other residents. Some of them asked what had happened, but he felt too stunned to reply. Frank had to hold Alex tight as his son was unsteady on his feet.

They waited in the apartment lobby, oblivious to the comings and goings around them. In a few minutes the ambulance arrived. Medics came and gave Alex a blanket and the two of them sat underneath it in the flashing blue and red lights of the emergency vehicles that now crowded the street.

Frank had not hugged Alex like that since he was ten or eleven. It seemed simultaneously years ago and only yesterday. They waited in a daze for the medics to stabilise the wounded stranger. Whoever he was, he had saved them from Kohl.

While they were waiting for the ambulance to leave to take Alex to the nearby hospital, Frank remembered the dossier. He went up to the apartment but it was now full of police and detectives carrying out forensic work, and they wouldn't let him in. Hübner came out and assured him they already had the dossier wrapped in an evidence bag.

'Once the ambulance has left, then we will have to

take you down to the police station. But use the phone here to call home first, if you like. Let your family know what's happened.'

Frank made a quick call home. When Gretchen came on the line, the whole room heard her cry out with relief. He wanted to cry too, but he felt embarrassed surrounded by all these police people.

Hübner came down with him to wait with Alex. When the ambulance men called over for Alex, Hübner put a hand on his shoulder. 'Don't worry about your father,' he said. 'We know what's been going on.'

Gretchen and Geli arrived at the hospital within half an hour of Frank's call. The doctor told them Alex was in shock and dehydrated, with bruises on his arm and wrists, and abrasions on his mouth. They would keep him in overnight but he was certain he would be fit to be discharged after breakfast the next morning.

Alex was especially pleased to have his family around him. Both of them stayed with him through the night. He slept fitfully, waking with a start several times, dreaming that he was back in the chair.

An ambulance took the three of them home the next morning. They immediately switched on the radio to listen to the news. A Red Army Faction terrorist, Ronald Sommer, had been arrested after having been shot by police in Kreuzberg last night. He was still in a critical condition. There was no mention of Kohl or the Ostermanns.

Hübner came round later that morning and they were all delighted to see Frank amble in after him.

'I'm all right,' said Frank. 'They're not going to hold me.' He seemed years younger and smiled quite naturally – something none of the family had seen since their arrival in West Berlin.

Hübner called for their attention. 'I have a few things to tell you but first we have to search your apartment.' A small team of technicians arrived. They found five minute listening devices concealed around the apartment, and photographed each in its hiding place before removing it. The Stasi had done an extremely professional job, explained Hübner. It was no wonder the Ostermanns couldn't find the bugs when they looked for them.

When the technicians left, Hübner stayed behind. First he asked them not to talk to the newspapers. This was a delicate matter, he said, and they wanted the enemy to know as little as possible about what had happened the night before. He also made it clear that if the story did come out, they would have to prosecute Frank Ostermann for industrial espionage.

For now, charges against Frank would be dropped. He had given them a thorough account of his actions in West Berlin and had obviously been acting under extreme duress. The fibre optics file had not been lost. The Stasi had not been able to make use of it. No actual harm had been done. His department were currently scrutinising the records of all Siemens employees in the West Berlin office, and interviewing them, to try to ascertain who else was working for the East Germans.

Siemens were not so forgiving. The BfV had explained that Frank was being blackmailed and that no details of their dossier had actually been taken to the East. But they had insisted on pressing charges, until the BfV had told them it was essential to keep the whole operation secret. It made everyone in the West look bad.

Kohl had escaped. For now, explained Hübner, the family could stay in their apartment. It might be expedient to move them out of Berlin where the Stasi could not abduct them so easily. But Hübner thought it unlikely this would happen. Through no fault of his own, Frank's cover had been blown. He had acted as they had instructed. This was an operation that had come to an end. His hunch was that they would leave him and his family alone.

Erich Kohl returned to Normannenstrasse to file his report. He wondered, a little queasily, how far he would be held responsible for the failure of this operation. He noted in his account how he had been able to get Frank Ostermann to steal the Siemens dossier and how everything had gone to plan until the intervention of the mysterious gunman. West Berlin radio news indicated the man was Ronald Sommer, a Red Army Faction terrorist. He was known to the International Sektion at Normannenstrasse.

Theissen called him into his office that morning for a thorough debriefing. 'Our Red Army Faction contacts tell us Sommer was acting alone,' he told Kohl. 'His girl-friend had been killed in a shoot-out with the police just before the February arrests. Sommer still believed it was you who had betrayed them.'

Kohl cursed. 'I knew I had hit him because he stopped chasing me. I should have gone back to finish him off.'

'He may not live.'

Theissen was being unusually cold with him, Kohl noticed. He suspected this would mean an end to his West German operations. It was a shame. He would miss what the West had to offer.

As Kohl opened the door to leave, Theissen spoke softly but clearly and gave a little wave. '*Sieg Heil, Herr Schneider.*'

Kohl's blood froze in his veins.

CHAPTER 36

The last thing Erich Kohl saw as he was frogmarched from his office was the smirk on his secretary's face. He had been several days now without a visitor to his basement cell and had nothing to do but sit in these sparse white walls and contemplate his fate. Would they despatch him with a single shot to the back of the neck – a blinding flash of agony and then eternal darkness. Or would they use the guillotine? He'd heard your head lived on for a few seconds, maybe even a minute after it had been cut off. He wondered how much it would hurt, falling from the lunette into the tin bucket.

Theissen had often mentioned the fate of Oleg Penkovsky – the Soviet Colonel caught spying for the West. His KGB colleagues had told Theissen he had been fed into a basement furnace, feet first. What a fine example to the rest of them, Theissen would chuckle, then remark that he hated traitors almost as much as he hated Nazis. Maybe Theissen had something equally imaginative lined up for him?

Ilse Grau arrived at Comrade Minister Erich Mielke's open door on the top floor of Building Number 1 with his breakfast. She was relieved to hear no answer when she knocked. She peeked round the door. His chair was empty. Sometimes the Comrade Minister would be absent for ten or fifteen minutes at that time of the morning. As instructed she proceeded to place his eggs, bread and coffee on the side of his desk. She also cast a quick eye on the documents that lay before her. One particularly caught her eye concerning Unterleutnant Erich Kohl – not least because Mielke had scrawled LIQUIDATE boldly at the bottom. She had no time to read more, but she knew Kohl. He was one of the more unpleasant customers at the canteen. She also knew a man in Blaschkoallee who paid her generously for any information she had gleaned from her day to day work at Normannenstrasse.

Alex had found Hübner's reassurances compelling, so he was acutely disappointed that Frank and Gretchen decided it would be safer for them all to leave Berlin and go to West Germany. Alex and Geli both argued forcefully that they should stay. 'We're settled here, we like it. And you like your job, Mutti,' said Geli.

'And it's Christmas,' said Alex. 'Wouldn't it be nice to spend Christmas here, without another upheaval. All those strangers in a new town to get to know.'

Frank was especially surprised that they were so keen to stay. 'Alex, you've been kidnapped. They said they could have you back in the East in an hour. Doesn't that worry you?'

Alex shrugged. 'Hübner's right. They're done with us. I want to stay here.'

But Frank and Gretchen were determined to go.

A few days before they intended to leave, Franz Hübner paid them another visit. Alex was slightly irritated to see him as he was glued to the television watching the *Apollo 17* moon landing and the American astronauts' excursions on their extraordinary Lunar Rover. Alex liked the fact that one of the crew, Harrison Schmitt, had a German name.

But Hübner had some good news. He told them the BfV understood that Kohl had been taken off Western Operations. He was hazy about what had happened to him, but he let the Ostermanns know that he certainly wouldn't be bothering them again. Besides, with Frank's cover blown, any further harassment would be purely vindictive. He was sure the Stasi had more important priorities for their agents in the West. It was enough to persuade Frank and Gretchen to stay.

Alex went to bed that evening feeling pleased. He did not want another upheaval in his life. But he found himself awake again in the early hours, thinking about Sophie Kirsch, and how she had betrayed him. Of course Frank had told him all about the Stasi and Kohl and the Siemens job. But Alex couldn't figure out why the Stasi would deliberately set them up to escape and then put their lives in danger with a shoot-out at the border. As his father said, Normannenstrasse was a vast place. Maybe one hand didn't know what the other hand was doing. Sophie could have tipped off one department, who arranged the ambush, without the other lot – the ones Frank was working with – knowing about it. He'd give anything to know what had really happened.

In the dead of night, when the traffic was quiet, he could still hear the guard dogs howling by the Wall. One day, he promised himself, he would move away from this scar on the landscape. The future had no boundaries.

CHAPTER 37

May 1973

Sophie Kirsch found the wide avenues by Treptower Park quite disconcerting. The occasional car that sped past startled her in a way it never used to. She supposed that feeling uncomfortable in the great outdoors was an inevitable consequence of ten months' confinement in the Youth Detention Wing at Hohenschönhausen. It was a warm spring day but she would not dream of going out without a hat. It would take several months for her prison haircut to grow out.

They did not usually shave the heads of the girls – that was too reminiscent of photographs in their history textbooks of prisoners in the Nazi concentration camps. But there had been a particularly tenacious outbreak of lice in the prison and drastic measures were called for. Actually, lice had been the least of Sophie's problems. The frequent isolation had been the worst part of her incarceration. Sophie had tried to keep sane by attempting to remember poems and stories. After days alone, broken only by the arrival of meals pushed through her cell door, she discovered she was able to recall whole pieces of music in great detail. It was almost like listening to them. She missed her cello and she missed her grandma's contraband records. But most of all she missed Alex Ostermann and the thought of what had happened to him was a daily torment.

The Stasi had come for her three days after Alex had told her he was going. All the gawpers in her apartment block had twitched their net curtains as she was taken away, and her parents had gone white with shame.

The knock at the door had come just as Sophie was scanning through the local paper. She read, with mounting alarm, that the Anti-Fascist Protection Barrier had been breached and two human traffickers, Albert Metzger and Heinz Amsel, had been shot dead. She was sure Alex and his family would have been caught up in all that. Had they been killed? Were they in prison? How would she ever find out? She remembered too clearly how Holger Vogel's family had been treated when he went missing.

'Why have you not reported the intentions of the border violator Alex Ostermann?' asked her interrogators as soon as she arrived in police custody. Hadn't it been made transparently clear to her that the only reason she had remained at liberty following the incident at the House of Ministries was so she could provide intelligence on negative-decadents at Treptower Polytechnic School. Sophie stuck to her story. She had no idea Alex Ostermann was going. She wanted to ask what had happened to him, but she was fearful of betraying herself with a slip of the tongue. Besides, whatever they told her would not be true.

In the weeks since her initial arrest at the House of

Ministries, Sophie had been making an effort to please them. But she had been careful to say nothing that would make Alex's life more difficult. She told them his trip to Hohenschönhausen had shaken him badly and provoked a dramatic reappraisal of his life. In his conversations with her, she imparted, he showed every indication of wanting to reform and become a useful member of the Republik. To keep them happy, she occasionally fed them titbits about Anton, and his disrespect for the Socialist Unity Party and the teachers at school. She hated herself for doing it, but told herself what she told them was harmless enough. She didn't know Anton was of no interest to the Stasi. He worked for them too.

Sophie spent her time in Hohenschönhausen wondering how she was going to make contact with Alex when she got out. If he was still alive. Maybe they'd all been murdered and the newspaper was keeping quiet about that? After a few months, another thought occurred to her. Alex had confided in her just before they went. It was too unlikely, surely, that the incident with Albert Metzger and Heinz Amsel would not have been connected with the Ostermanns. How did the Stasi know they were going? Would Alex think it was her who had betrayed them?

Posting a letter was out of the question. Even if she knew where to send it, she was sure the Stasi would read it before the end of the day. Then she remembered Grandma Ostermann. She had gone to see her once with him. If she could remember where she lived, perhaps Sophie could persuade her to take a message out for her.

And now, here she was, three days out of prison, trying to remember which side street of Treptower Park would take her to Alex's grandma's apartment. The corner of Klingerstrasse looked familiar so she walked down it to Leiblstrasse, and there it was. The dingy white block with the balconies. His grandma, she remembered, lived just above the main entrance. It seemed half a lifetime away, when they had last been there.

Sophie walked up the red lino staircase and, heart in mouth, knocked twice on the door. She heard shuffling and a bolt being drawn back. The door opened a crack.

'*Ja?*' came an impatient voice she recognised at once. 'What do you want?'

'Frau Ostermann, it's me, Sophie. Alex's friend. Can I talk to you?'

'Go away,' she said and closed the door. Frank and Gretchen had told her they thought she might have betrayed them.

Sophie leaned towards the door and begged. 'Please. I promise I will only keep you a moment.'

Grandma Ostermann relented. The door opened again.

'Can I come in?' asked Sophie.

They stood in the hall. The apartment was fusty and needed a good dusting. 'Are you managing OK without Frank and Gretchen?' Sophie asked.

'What do you want?' said Grandma impatiently.

'I want to know what happened to Alex and his family?' Sophie blurted out.

Grandma Ostermann was instantly wary. 'I know you are not to be trusted.'

Sophie's face lit up. They were alive; they must be. There was obviously no bad news. And 'I don't know' would have meant she had not heard and there had been no contact. She must have been able to talk to them. Otherwise why would she say that?

Sophie took her hand. She could barely contain her glee. Tears were brimming in her eyes. She was grinning madly. 'Grandma Ostermann, I will ask you no more questions!' She pulled a plain white envelope from her pocket. She was so frightened of the Stasi finding out what she intended to do she had not addressed it. 'Can I leave a letter here for you to take to Alex?'

Grandma Ostermann was confused. She looked at the joy and relief in Sophie's face and her hostility melted a little. She liked to think she was a fine judge of human behaviour and unless Sophie Kirsch was a world-class actor, she seemed genuinely elated that Alex was still alive.

But she still wasn't certain. 'They think you betrayed them, you know,' she said.

Sophie nodded. Her elation began to fade. 'I feared as much but all I can do is swear to you I didn't. I don't know what I can do to make you, or them, believe me. But can I ask you . . .'

Grandma Ostermann put a hand firmly on hers. 'No more questions.' She shook her head. 'Why have you not come to see me before?' she asked.

Sophie pulled her hat from her head, revealing her prison haircut. 'I've just come out of Hohenschönhausen.'

Grandma Ostermann nodded, and squeezed Sophie's hand. 'Here is what we will do,' she whispered. 'Leave your message in my letter box in the hall. I may or may not pick it up.' She winked as she spoke. 'Now off you go.'

Sophie almost skipped down the street back to her parents' apartment where she had arranged to collect some clothes. She had not felt this happy since the night Alex had walked her home from Greifswalder Strasse. She hoped her letter would reach him. It was simple enough. She told Alex she thought of him often. She had just spent ten months in Hohenschönhausen but she was all right. Auntie Rosemarie had taken her in as her parents had disowned her. She did not want Alex to think she had betrayed him and maybe, one day, they would see each other again. But even if the letter never did reach him, Grandma Ostermann had accepted it. That could only mean one thing. They had got away.

Three weeks later, Alex Ostermann returned home after midnight on the evening he finally got to see Led Zeppelin at the Deutschlandhalle in Berlin. They played 'Black Dog' three numbers in and Alex thought he had died and gone to heaven. He sat down at the kitchen table to drink a small glass of milk, his ears still ringing from the volume of the concert, and took his beige concert ticket from his shirt pocket. It was tattered and damp with sweat, but Alex wanted to put it somewhere where he would never ever lose it. Among the usual domestic clutter on the table, his eyes alighted on a plain white envelope. His mother had written on it in pencil: *Alex – Grandma brought this for you.*

INSPIRATION AND SOURCES

In the winter of 2008 I visited Prague to research my book *The Cabinet of Curiosities* and spent an evening in a scruffy bar listening to a Czech rock band. I got talking with a group of locals there who would have been teenagers in the early 1970s. They told me how important rock music had been to them as a symbol of freedom and a way of life forbidden to them by the Communist regime that controlled their country at that time.

I also read *Stasiland*, Anna Funder's fascinating book about life in the DDR, and watched the brilliant film *The Lives of Others* by Florian Henckel von Donnersmarck. It brought home to me how lucky I had been to grow up in a culture which allowed its citizens to have their own opinions and listen to whatever music they liked.

In *Sektion 20* I am trying to bring to life an era of East German history that many people alive today remember clearly. I have tried to depict the society and the events that transpire here as accurately as possible. Whilst researching the book, I encountered widely differing accounts of 'what it was really like' to be a citizen of the DDR. Some people had a rough time, suffered greatly and even died at the hands of the Stasi. Other people regarded the Stasi as incompetent clowns and were allowed to leave the country with barely a murmur of objection. I have also not forgotten that many former citizens of the DDR feel a great nostalgia for the security and sense of purpose the regime offered. The Western way of life has its myriad imperfections too – and I hope this comes over in my story.

For those readers who would like to learn more about the DDR, I can recommend a visit to the DDR Museum on Karl-Liebknecht-Strasse in Berlin – a commercial enterprise packed to the brim with East German memorabilia. The magnificent Deutsches Historisches Museum, a short stroll away on Unter den Linden, is a more traditional museum which has a fascinating Cold War era gallery. Captions for all their exhibits are in German and English.

The BBC series *The Lost World of Communism*, available on DVD, has an intriguing episode about East Germany. Margaret Fulbrook's book *The People's State* (Yale University Press, 2005) is also a very readable introduction.

The Rainier-Wolfcastle-like line on page 208 attributed to one of Lily Weber's swimming coaches – 'My girls have come to Munich to swim, not sing' – is based on a remark one East German swimming coach made four years later at the Montreal Olympics.

Finally, the early 1970s produced some great rock music. If you don't know them, you might like to track down the songs that crop up in the story and have a listen. They still sound pretty good forty years later!

ACKNOWLEDGEMENTS

As ever, my thanks are due to my valued editors, Ele Fountain and Isabel Ford, who helped me shape and polish the story, Diana Hickman, who proofread, and Dilys Dowswell, who read through my first drafts. Christian Staufenbiel of Cambridge University Library kindly read and commented on the manuscript. Thank you too to my agent Charlie Viney, and Jenny and Josie Dowswell, and Kate Clarke and Black Sheep for the evocative cover.

When I visited Berlin to research the book, I was looked after marvellously by Kati Hertzsch. My thanks also to Dorit Engelhardt and Anna von Hahn for their advice and hospitality. I was also lucky enough to meet Wolfgang Grossman, who spent his childhood and teenage years as a citizen of the DDR. We spent a brilliant day wandering the streets of Berlin together. Although his life turned out quite differently from Alex's, talking to Wolfgang was a great inspiration.

CHAPTER 1

Warsaw
August 2, 1941

Piotr Bruck shivered in the cold as he waited with twenty or so other naked boys in the long draughty corridor. He carried his clothes in an untidy bundle and hugged them close to his chest to try to keep warm. The late summer day was overcast and the rain had not let up since daybreak. He could see the goose pimples on the scrawny shoulder of the boy in front. That boy was shivering too, maybe from cold, maybe from fear. Two men in starched white coats sat at a table at the front of the line. They were giving each boy a cursory examination with strange-looking instruments. Some boys were sent to the room at the left of the table. Others were curtly dismissed to the room at the right.

Piotr and the other boys had been ordered to be silent and not look around. He willed his eyes to stay firmly fixed forward. So strong was Piotr's fear, he felt almost detached from his body. Every movement he made seemed unnatural, forced. The only thing keeping him in the here and now was a desperate ache in his bladder. Piotr knew there was no point asking for permission to use the lavatory. When the soldiers had descended on the orphanage to hustle the boys from their beds and into a waiting van, he had asked to go. But he got a sharp cuff round the ear for talking out of turn.

The soldiers had first come to the orphanage two

weeks ago. They had been back several times since. Sometimes they took boys, sometimes girls. Some of the boys in Piotr's overcrowded dormitory had been glad to see them go: 'More food for us, more room too, what's the problem?' said one. Only a few of the children came back. Those willing to tell what had happened had muttered something about being photographed and measured.

Now, just ahead in the corridor, Piotr could see several soldiers in black uniforms. The sort with lightning insignia on the collars. Some had dogs – fierce Alsatians who strained restlessly at their chain leashes. He had seen men like this before. They had come to his village during the fighting. He had seen first-hand what they were capable of.

There was another man watching them. He wore the same lightning insignia as the soldiers, but his was bold and large on the breast pocket of his white coat. He stood close to Piotr, tall and commanding, arms held behind his back, overseeing this mysterious procedure. When he turned around, Piotr noticed he carried a short leather riding whip. The man's dark hair flopped lankly over the top of his head, but it was shaved at the sides, in the German style, a good seven or eight centimetres above the ears.

Observing the boys through black-rimmed spectacles he would nod or shake his head as his eyes passed along the line. Most of the boys, Piotr noticed, were blond like him, although a few had darker hair.

The man had the self-assured air of a doctor, but what he reminded Piotr of most was a farmer, examining his pigs and wondering which would fetch the best price at the village market. He caught Piotr staring and tutted impatiently through tight, thin lips, signalling for him to look to the front with a brisk, semicircular motion of his index finger.

Now Piotr was only three rows from the table, and could hear snippets of the conversation between the two men there. 'Why was this one brought in?' Then louder to the boy before him. 'To the right, quick, before you feel my boot up your arse.'

Piotr edged forward. He could see the room to the right led directly to another corridor and an open door that led outside. No wonder there was such a draught. Beyond was a covered wagon where he glimpsed sullen young faces and guards with bayonets on their rifles. He felt another sharp slap to the back of his head. 'Eyes forward!' yelled a soldier. Piotr thought he was going to wet himself, he was so terrified.

On the table was a large box file. Stencilled on it in bold black letters were the words:

RACE AND SETTLEMENT MAIN OFFICE

Now Piotr was at the front of the queue praying hard not to be sent to the room on the right. One of the men in the starched white coats was looking directly at him. He smiled and turned to his companion who was reaching for a strange device that reminded Piotr of a pair of spindly pincers. There were several of these on the table. They looked like sinister medical instruments, but their purpose was not to extend or hold open human orifices or surgical incisions. These pincers had centimetre measurements indented along their polished steel edges.

'We hardly need to bother,' he said to his companion. 'He looks just like that boy in the *Hitler-Jugend* poster.'

They set the pincers either side of his ears, taking swift measurements of his face. The man indicated he should go to the room on the left with a smile. Piotr scurried in. There, other boys were dressed and waiting. As his fear subsided, he felt foolish standing there naked, clutching his clothes. There were no soldiers here, just two nurses, one stout and maternal, the other young and petite. Piotr blushed crimson. He saw a door marked *Herren* and dashed inside.

The ache in his bladder gone, Piotr felt light-headed with relief. They had not sent him to the room on the right and the covered wagon. He was here with the nurses. There was a table with biscuits, and tumblers and a jug of water. He found a spot over by the window and hurriedly dressed. He had arrived at the orphanage with only the clothes he stood up in and these were a second set they had given him. He sometimes wondered who his grubby pullover had belonged to and hoped its previous owner had grown out of it rather than died.

Piotr looked around at the other boys here with him. He recognised several faces but there was no one here he would call a friend.

Outside in the corridor he heard the scrape of wood on polished floor. The table was being folded away. The selection was over. The last few boys quickly dressed as the older nurse clapped her hands to call everyone to attention.

'Children,' she said in a rasping German accent, stumbling clumsily round the Polish words. 'Very important gentleman here to talk. Who speak German?'

No one came forward.

'Come now,' she smiled. 'Do not be shy.'

Piotr could sense that this woman meant him no harm. He stepped forward, and addressed her in fluent German.

'Well, you are a clever one,' she replied in German, putting a chubby arm around his shoulder. 'Where did you learn to speak like that?'

'My parents, miss,' said Piotr. 'They both speak –' Then he stopped and his voice faltered. 'They both spoke German.'

The nurse hugged him harder as he fought back tears. No one had treated him this kindly at the orphanage.

'Now who are you, mein Junge?' she said. Between sobs he blurted out his name.

'Pull yourself together, young Piotr,' she whispered in German. 'The Doktor is not the most patient fellow.'

The tall, dark-haired man Piotr had seen earlier strolled into the room. He stood close to the nurse and asked her which of the boys spoke German. 'Just give me a moment with this one,' she said. She turned back to Piotr and said gently, 'Now dry those eyes. I want you to tell these children what the Doktor says.'

She pinched his cheek and Piotr stood nervously at the front of the room, waiting for the man to begin talking.

He spoke loudly, in short, clear sentences, allowing Piotr time to translate.

'My name is Doktor Fischer . . . I have something very special to tell you . . . You boys have been chosen as candidates . . . for the honour of being reclaimed by the German National Community . . . You will undergo further examinations . . . to establish your racial value . . .

273

and whether or not you are worthy of such an honour
. . . Some of you will fail and be sent back to your own
people.'

He paused, looking them over like a stern school –
teacher.

'Those of you who are judged to be *Volksdeutsche* – of
German blood – will be taken to the Fatherland . . . and
found good German homes and German families.'

Piotr felt a glimmer of excitement, but as the other
boys listened their eyes grew wide with shock. The room
fell silent. Doktor Fischer turned on his heels and was
gone. Then there was uproar – crying and angry
shouting. Immediately, the Doktor sprang back into the
room and cracked his whip against the door frame. Two
soldiers stood behind him.

'How dare you react with such ingratitude. You will
assist my staff in this process,' he yelled and the noise
subsided instantly. 'And you will not want to be one of
those left behind.'

Piotr shouted out these final remarks in Polish. He was
too preoccupied trying to translate this stream of words
to notice an angry boy walking purposefully towards
him. The boy punched him hard on the side of the head
and knocked him to the floor. 'Traitor,' he spat, as he was
dragged away by a soldier.

'A heart-racing and hugely impressive thriller'
The Bookseller

About the author

A former senior editor with Usborne Publishing, Paul Dowswell is now a full-time author. He has written over 60 books, including *Ausländer*, nominated for the Carnegie Medal, the Red House Children's Book Award and the Booktrust Teenage Prize. Paul lives in Wolverhampton with his family.